TO CADEN AND COLE—

I HOPE YOU LIKE
DRAGONS!

Gwendolyn
and the
Seeds of Destiny

Roy Sakelson

For Claire
You're going to do great things.

CONTENTS

Everything that exists is in a manner
the seed of that which will be.

— Marcus Aurelius
The Meditations

.

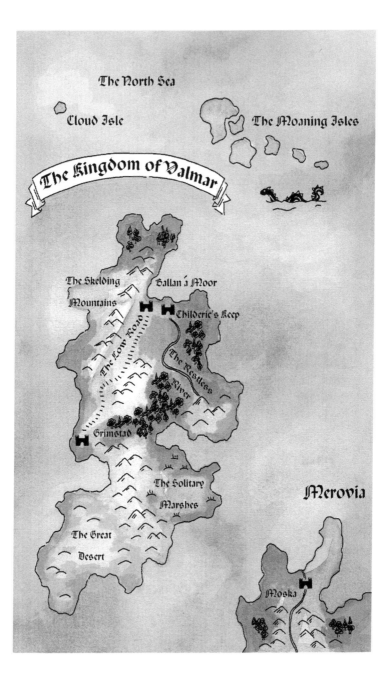

The North Sea

Cloud Isle

The Moaning Isles

The Kingdom of Valmar

The Skelding
Mountains

Ballan's Moor

Childeric's Keep

The Low Road

The Restless River

Grimstad

The Solitary

Marshes

The Great

Desert

Merovia

Moska

PROLOGUE:
CHILDERIC'S CURSE

The world was once filled with monsters. At least, that's what you would call them if you saw them today. They weren't the imaginary monsters that some children (and even adults) fear may be hiding under beds. Nor did they delight in making strange noises from behind closed doors. No, these creatures had grander ambitions for they lived in a grander age—an age defined by hardship, sacrifice, and above all, courage.

Some of these monsters were good and some were evil. Many of them, like us, were a mixture of both. If they differed from you and me in an important way, however, it would be this: they didn't doubt for a moment who or what they were or whether or not they belonged in the world. They did not spend their nights, as some do, doubting their purpose, their worth, or their way of life. These creatures simply acted according to their nature. If that made them more fortunate than we are—or less so—you will have to decide for yourself.

Long ago, when our ancestors were new to this world, they discovered these monsters. They met the giants first, learning from them how to work with metal and stone. With the giants' help, men quickly mastered the art of building strong castles and crafting iron weapons. As men pushed into the forests, they met the centaurs, who loved to wander along narrow, leaf-laden paths. Though centaurs generally kept to themselves, they took pity on the short lives of men, and patiently taught them geometry and astronomy. Using this knowledge, men learned to sail the seas, trading with distant countries and fishing far from shore.

Perhaps most impressive of all, gryphons, who were naturally very solemn, flew down from the mountain peaks where they made their nests to instruct men in the arts of medicine and herbology. (For those of you who have been forced to drink cod liver oil, you can thank the gryphons, for they taught men of its healing properties.) What was a gryphon, you ask? Imagine a beast with the body of a lion but with the head and wings of an eagle. A gryphon could fly faster than the wind and was deadly to his foes—but you would never mistake the creature for a bird. Those unfortunate enough to have met a gryphon in battle always wondered which was worse: trying to avoid the beast's cruel claws or his razor sharp beak. It was rare to see a gryphon—even in ancient times. You would never have a more loyal ally, however, if one chose you as a friend.

Other creatures our ancestors met in the early days, I'm afraid, were simply wicked. These included ogres, who mainly lived alone in caves or under bridges, gnawing on the bones of ill-fated men who were unlucky enough to meet them alone in the wild. (This is why we still think of monsters hiding in dark places.) In fact, ogres had become so solitary that they had forgotten the art of speech, and grew hairy like animals. Some say that ogres were once a race of giants, but that they had slowly changed, becoming wilder and their hearts harder after centuries of living alone in the shadows.

Trolls, on the other hand, were more social than ogres (though no less wicked) and preferred to live in tunnels deep in the mountains. Over time, they developed excellent vision, and could see in the dark. Though they hated sunlight—it was too bright for eyes grown accustomed to darkness—trolls quite enjoyed the moonlight. In fact, they worshipped the moon, for its lonely, pock-marked face in a sea of darkness reminded them of themselves. When the moon was full, the trolls would climb out of their holes by the hundreds and dance for hours bathed in the moon's soft, silver light. The sound of their stomping feet and rhythmic chanting would fill the mountain passes and distant valleys below, causing men to lock their doors and stoke their hearth fires. For trolls weren't very fond of fire, though they used it on occasion to suit their purposes.

There was nothing, however, more feared than dragons. These scaly beasts lived—well, they lived anywhere they pleased—but they often chose dark, closed spaces so that they could more easily keep an eye on their treasure. As you may know, dragons were greedy, and had a passion for precious stones. They also loved to collect the weapons of those they killed, keeping them as trophies. A successful dragon could have hundreds of swords, shields, axes, and bows from men brave or foolish enough to do battle with him.

Above all things, however, dragons loved gold. They loved to touch it, smell it, and sleep in it, settling into a pile of gold coins the way a bird settles into his nest. Where did dragons get their treasure? I'm afraid they stole it—mostly from men. For men also shared the dragons' narrowing lust for gold. The beasts could breathe fire and their skin was thicker than any shield. They smelled of sulphur. What isn't so well known, however, is that dragons could live for centuries. As a result, they often grew to be very cunning and intelligent, and some were even skilled in the art of magic.

Unfortunately, the knowledge they gained from experience didn't make them any kinder or more compassionate toward men or any other creature. (Intelligence and kindness don't always go hand in hand, as you may have already learned.) Most of all, dragons caused fear in all living things—except perhaps in very brave gryphons—making it very difficult to think clearly when one stood before you or hovered overhead.

***

This story begins with a young king who was lucky enough to meet a gryphon, unlucky enough to anger a dragon, and crafty enough to leave a mysterious legacy that would cause his great-grandchildren to guess at his secrets. The king's name was Childeric, and he ruled over a kingdom in the northern part of Valmar, a small island that has since been lost to time.

Valmar was a beautiful place. In the northern part of the island, where men lived, fields of wild flowers hummed with bees during summer. Clear rivers thick with salmon meandered through forests of oak and beech and pine. Small farms and hamlets dotted green valleys, yellow plains, and the rocky-soiled foothills. Far away to the southwest lay the Great Desert where, blown by the fierce ocean breeze, the sand dunes shifted restlessly, regularly remaking the landscape the way a potter reshapes wet clay. To the southeast sat the Solitary Marshes, swarming with deadly insects, poisonous frogs, hungry alligators—and worse things that didn't like to be seen above the murky waters. Finally, a range of snow-capped mountains—the Skeldings—ran up the island like a great spine from north to south, hiding forgotten volcanoes deep below the earth.

Childeric was just returning from an unsuccessful afternoon of hunting in the forest at dusk when he heard a deep-throated cry. Spurring his horse onward, he came to a clearing and saw a young giant, about twelve feet tall, being attacked by two trolls. How did he know the giant was young? Well, you see, the three creatures were all about the same size. If the giant had been fully mature, he would have stood about a head taller than the trolls. Unfortunately for the giant, the others were armed with cruel-looking scimitars while he was without a weapon. (Trolls never did favor a fair fight.) The larger of the two trolls wore an eye-patch that covered part of his hideous, green face, while the other had a bone through his nose, apparently on purpose. Now, the two converged upon the giant slowly, with the curved blades of their scimitars pointed at him.

The poor giant was clearly not ready for this fight. He had been innocently picking blueberries when the trolls stepped out from behind some trees. Now, the berries lay scattered under his feet as he held out the basket in front of him like a shield, blinking rapidly as he tried to decide what to do next. The trolls, for their part, were not impressed. They wanted to capture him quickly so that they could return to the mountains with him before dawn.

Suddenly, the one-eyed troll lunged forward with his scimitar. The giant dodged the brunt of the blow, but the blade still grazed his shoulder, drawing blood.

"Be careful!" grunted the smaller troll. "We need him alive!"

"We've already tried it your way!" shouted the other, and attacked again. Before his stroke fell, however, an arrow came whizzing out of the forest and buried itself in the one-eyed troll's throat. The beast fell backwards, clutching at the arrow as he gasped for breath, twitching a few times before he died. The giant and the other troll looked up in surprise. Childeric jumped off his horse, stepped into the clearing, and fit another arrow on his bowstring. He had never met a giant or a troll before but he didn't need to be told which side to take.

Seeing his companion dead, the smaller troll forgot the giant for a moment. Raising his weapon in both hands, he charged Childeric, snarling as he came. The young king, however, expected this. He raised his bow carefully, aiming at the troll's right eye, and let his arrow fly.

He missed.

Instantly, the troll was upon him. Childeric stumbled backwards and raised his bow to ward off the inevitable blow, knowing he would probably not survive. The stroke, however, never fell. Instead, the troll's eyes grew wide and his mouth slack as the creature paused. Then he crashed forward, bowling over Childeric in the process, before he lay still.

The giant had seized the one-eyed troll's weapon and stabbed him from behind when the beast was attacking the young king. Now, the giant pulled Childeric to his feet and set him down as one would a small child.

"I am in your debt," said the giant, grinning broadly and revealing a mouth full of sharp teeth. (Childeric wasn't alarmed by this, however, because he knew that all giants are, strangely enough, vegetarians.)

"I believe we are even," he replied, looking at the dead troll that had nearly beheaded him, before returning the giant's smile.

The giant shook his head. "No," he declared, ruefully. "I would have been killed—or even worse—captured by these horrible creatures had it not been for your bravery. Thank you."

Childeric swept his cloak aside and bowed. "Childeric, king of Valmar, at your service."

The giant also bowed. "Ollom, prince of the Western Giants, at yours."

Childeric was surprised. The Western Giants were rarely seen this far north. They mostly kept to themselves, living in a mighty castle called Grimstad that had stood for generations in the mountains to the southwest.

"What did they want with you?" asked Childeric.

"I don't know," responded Ollom. "I was out gathering blueberries when they attacked." He held up his ruined basket and looked down disappointedly at its scattered contents. "As you may know, we regard berries as a delicacy, and I came a bit farther than normal in search of them."

"It's been years since trolls have been seen in this forest," said Childeric, frowning. "If I had known they had grown so bold, I would not have risked hunting alone."

"It concerns us too," said the giant grimly. "They grow in strength and number in the mountains, and we now guard passes that were once safe. Still, I was unwise to be travelling without my spear—especially during a full moon."

Childeric realized it would be dark soon. He asked the giant if he would like to return to the castle and spend the night. Ollom laughed. "I doubt you have a room large enough to hold me! In any case, I must decline. My father will already be wondering what's become of me. Farewell, Childeric of Valmar! If I can ever repay you, I will!" Before Childeric could ask him to reconsider, the giant turned and disappeared into the forest.

***

A few months later Childeric was once again travelling on horseback far from home. This time, however, his chief steward, Goran, accompanied him. They were both armed with swords and crossbows in case they should meet any trolls. The two men were surveying some land near the uninhabited foothills on Valmar's southern border, looking for a spot to plant a vineyard. The valley near the castle was already cultivated, but they both thought grapes could grow well at a higher elevation, even in rocky soil. Childeric slowed his horse and looked up at the foothills.

"Clearing the trees and bushes will take some work, my lord," said Goran, not realizing that the king had fallen behind. "But it will be well worth it." Noticing the king's absence, he circled back and then wrinkled his nose. Something stank. "Where is that smell coming from?" he asked, covering his nose with his sleeve and scanning the surrounding countryside. "Could it be a dead animal?"

"I'm not sure," said Childeric, looking closely at a grove of trees. Then he saw it. A large cave sat nestled in the hillside, obscured by many bushes and several large oaks. As they drew closer, the smell grew worse. Childeric dismounted. "Wait here."

Pushing past the undergrowth, he ambled toward the cave's entrance and sniffed again. Yes, the cave was definitely the source of the odor. He took a few more steps and noticed the scorched, blackened walls on either side of him. The markings were much too large to be made by a campfire. "A dragon's lair!" he whispered to himself in wonder. "Is it possible?" Childeric had always been taught to avoid the mountains, for this was where many strange creatures made their homes. But he knew he was still relatively safe in the foothills—and the sun was still high in the sky. There was no need to fear trolls or ogres out in the open at this time of day. Of course, dragons were a different matter. Still, he had never heard of a dragon's lair in Valmar.

He listened for any hint of movement at the mouth of the cave before deciding that it was empty. Then, drawing his sword, he ventured into the darkness. Why? Perhaps he was braver than most men—or greedier. For he knew that where there are dragons, there is gold. Ruling over a modest kingdom, Childeric could always use more of that. Surely a dragon wouldn't miss a few coins? And what sort of king would he be if he weren't ambitious?

As he walked into the cave, his stomach tightened in fear. There was no doubting it was indeed a dragon's lair. In addition to the scorch marks on the walls, bones littered the stone floor and, of course, it stank worse than ever. Childeric temporarily forgot his fear, however, when he saw more riches than he had dared to imagine. Dimly concealed by the cave's shadows lay piles and piles of gold. In addition, there were smaller piles of gemstones. Scattered elsewhere he saw rings, amulets, swords, and other objects he couldn't even recognize. If he had been more careful or had known more about dragons, however, he would have known that this lair was fairly new. A well-established dragon would have had ten times this amount. But to Childeric, the king of a small island with an equally small treasury, it was a fortune.

Gripped by a sudden madness, he could not resist jumping into the pile of gold nearest him, wading into it, and picking up large handfuls of the stuff as it slipped through his fingers. He smiled. First, he would build a navy. That would allow him to establish stronger trading ties to the Moaning Isles without fearing pirates. He could also pay for a larger army, which in turn could drive the troublesome trolls further south, toward the giants. Let Grimstad deal with them! His farmers would now be able to cultivate much more of the island's fertile valleys. And of course he needed a new castle—not the modest structure he had now. He wanted a grand castle with spires that would challenge the sun itself.

As he imagined himself ruling over a large empire, with emissaries from distant kingdoms bringing him tokens of tribute, a gleam of green light caught his eye at the very back of the cave. He sheathed his sword and walked deeper into the darkness where he discovered a green stone hidden behind a rocky crag. It was about the size of a watermelon and it sparkled like a star in the night sky. He touched it, admiring its smoothness. To his surprise, he felt a thrill of warmth go up his fingers. In a moment, the feeling spread to his arm and then to the rest of his body. It was a very pleasant feeling, almost electric. Just as quickly as it had come, however, the feeling disappeared.

His eyes widened as he admired the stone. "I've never seen a jewel this large before," he thought to himself. "It must be priceless." Then his thoughts grew suspicious. What if Goran were to secretly return to this cave and take some of the gold for himself? For a moment, Childeric reproached himself for such a thought. He had never known his steward to be anything but faithful and true. However, the risks were too high. He could not trust any man in his kingdom with the knowledge of the cave's whereabouts until he had more time to think. Still, he would be sorry to lose so precious a jewel as he now held. Where had the dragon found it?

The dragon! How could he have forgotten! How would he ever succeed in taking all of the gold back to his castle? Even if he managed it, the dragon would surely come to reclaim the treasure. Another thought occurred to him. What if the dragon was on his way back to the cave at this very moment? Childeric had already lingered too long. But he couldn't leave empty-handed.

He picked up the sparkling green stone and found it surprisingly heavy. Nevertheless, he staggered out of the cave with it much to his steward's wonder, claiming that it was all he had found. Then, with Goran's help, he tied it to the back of his horse.

"What do you think it is?" asked Goran, marveling at the king's find but glad to be leaving behind the horrible stench as they galloped back to the castle.

"Who knows?" replied Childeric, smiling like a child on Christmas morning. "For the moment, I'll call it a souvenir!"

***

That night, Childeric awoke to the unmistakable sound of a dragon's roar. It was distant, but the terrible noise still caused him to sit up in bed and shake with fright. He ran to the window and looked out from his tower to the southern mountains beyond. He could see nothing but the moon in the night sky. He looked down at the large town below. All appeared calm. Outside and below his window, a few torches on the castle's ramparts burned brightly to aid the guards on duty. He could neither see nor hear anything more.

"Perhaps it was only a dream," he thought, settling back into bed. Just as he had begun to convince himself that he was imagining things, he heard the roar again. Then he noticed the green stone sitting in the corner of his bedroom, washed in pale moonlight. "Childeric, you fool!" he thought frantically. "What have you done?"

The dragon roared a third time. The sound was definitely coming from the mountains. He quickly pulled on his clothes and boots, and snatched up the stone which somehow felt lighter. Strangely, his hands and arms grew warm, just as they had earlier that day. This time, however, the warmth grew into a burning sensation. Ignoring the pain, he ran downstairs and outside into the courtyard, cradling it carefully. Fortunately, the moon was full and he saw his destination. It was the courtyard's main well, surrounded by six pillars that supported a dome directly overhead to shade those who used it to supply the castle with water.

More of the guards were gathered together now on the ramparts. They were all looking toward the mountains and murmuring to one another. None saw the king emerge from the doorway below and hasten to the center of the courtyard. Lifting the stone, Childeric pushed it over the well's edge and watched it disappear into the darkness below. He closed his eyes in relief and slid to the ground, letting out a long, slow breath. The well was very deep, he remembered. In the morning, this would all seem like a dream.

"I'm afraid it's too late for that," croaked a strange voice.

Childeric opened his eyes and saw a gryphon standing in front of him. He cried out and tried to rise but slipped and fell backwards on the cold stone. He had never seen a gryphon before. In fact, he was not even sure what he was staring at until he remembered his grandfather's description of one long ago. The beast had folded his great, feathered wings but they still seemed to span the entire courtyard. Though it was dark, the moonlight showed the brilliant red and yellow plumage that covered the gryphon's head and neck. Childeric would have marveled at the creature's beauty if he had not been so frightened by his fierce expression. The beast took a step toward him and the young king noticed for the first time his large claws that gripped the cobblestones.

"There is little time," the gryphon continued, calmly. "Cynder will be here soon."

"Cynder?" said Childeric, confused.

"That is the dragon's name," he explained. "A particularly nasty one, too. You must warn your people to flee this place. Otherwise, they will not survive the night."

Childeric could see the flicker of candlelight in more and more of the castle's windows. Clearly, others had heard the dragon's roar and were now stirring. What would they think if they knew he had stolen from a dragon? That he was the cause of this terror? Fear gripped his heart. But Childeric was still a king. Now that he had gotten over the shock of the gryphon's sudden appearance, he resented being told what to do.

"Why should we flee?" he asked defensively, rising to his feet. His hand would have gone to his sword hilt, but he realized that he had none. "I have done nothing wrong! Who are you to command a king?"

Childeric knew immediately that this was a very unwise thing to say to a gryphon. The creature's eyes flashed and he made a low sound in his throat as he took another step toward Childeric. "You have stolen a dragon's seed," the gryphon said, angrily. "You are a fool to deny it just as you were a fool to take it." Childeric was about to demand how the gryphon knew this but he was interrupted by the dragon's roar. It sounded closer.

Fear can sometimes cause us to deny the obvious. It can, however, also force us to see things as they are. In Childeric's case, the gryphon's words—combined with the dragon's roar—made him understand the hopelessness of his situation. He realized that his decision to trespass into the dragon's lair could very well cost everyone their lives. Then Childeric did a very wise thing. He told the truth.

"You are right," he admitted. "I am sorry for insulting you. I will tell my people to flee to the woods immediately." He started to run back to the castle. Then he stopped and turned. "What is your name?"

"Men call me Eldon," replied the gryphon. "I will help you if I can, though you have done nothing to deserve it. Now go!" The beast unfolded his giant wings and leaped into the air. Childeric saw his majestic silhouette against the moon as the gryphon streaked away south.

Childeric ran to the guard tower and ordered his men to sound the alarm. They were to quickly escort everyone from the castle and town into the forest. There, they were to divide into small groups, making no sound, and remain under the forest's dense foliage until the danger passed. He knew it wasn't a very good plan but there was no time for a better one.

A short time later, hundreds of frightened people were running into the nearby woods with what few possessions they could carry, directed by Childeric's knights. The young king knew it was no use trying to defend the place. A dragon could smash wood and stone the way a child knocks down a sand castle. Childeric shuddered at the thought, and concentrated on helping his people reach safety. The work, however, could only distract him for a short time. Soon, he saw something dark and horrible approaching in the early morning light.

Cynder had come.

The beast was in such a rage that he made no attempt to surprise them. Instead, the dragon screamed in fury while still a mile away, causing those who heard him to cover their ears or cower in fright. As he drew nearer, his wings beat the air with such force that wooden shingles peeled off the roofs in the town below the castle. Peering out from behind a tree at the edge of the forest, Childeric noticed the dragon's bright, yellow eyes. Even from a distance, they glowed with a strange, hypnotic radiance. "Come out where I can see you," the creature seemed to say. "I will give you a quick death." With an effort, Childeric looked away, focusing instead on the stragglers running across the field to the forest's edge.

"Hurry!" he yelled as he ran out to help an old woman who was struggling to carry a hen. "You must hurry!" The rest of the terrified peasants, however, needed no encouragement. They sprinted toward Childeric as the dragon dove toward the village, dousing the buildings below with his fiery breath. Several houses burst into flame. The beast rose into the air and swung his great tail, smashing a large section of the castle's north wall before wheeling about and torching the royal stables.

As Childeric witnessed the dragon's destruction from the forest's edge, he wept. A king was responsible for protecting his people but he had brought this ruin to their very doorstep. For what? A stone? A souvenir? Even if they endured the dragon's wrath, how would they survive the winter with no shelter?

Then Childeric felt the ground shake. He looked up, expecting to see more of the castle crumbling as a result of the dragon's attack. But the creature had not landed. Cynder still hovered over the castle, raining down fire from above. If not the dragon, what could possibly make the earth tremble?

He gasped at what he saw next.

Giants. Dozens of giants were marching toward the castle. Was it possible? Clad in armor and carrying enormous shields and spears, they emerged from the forest, their faces grim but determined. Childeric guessed there must have been about forty of them. He looked more closely, and saw the familiar face of Ollom, the young giant whom he had helped, leading the charge.

Cynder saw them too. The dragon soared high into the air and roared. Then he attacked, diving towards them, breathing fire as he descended. Before the dragon could reach the giants, however, something large and feathered streaked directly into his path. Eldon! The gryphon had momentarily distracted the dragon, slashing at the beast's head. Finally, Childeric understood. The gryphon must have roused the giants, knowing the dragon would come to take his revenge. But how did the giants reach the castle so quickly? And why would they help him?

There was no time to ponder these questions as he watched the dragon and gryphon collide. Eldon had caught Cynder by surprise with a kick to the ribs, knocking the dragon backwards. However, Cynder beat his wings furiously and soon recovered, breathing fire at the gryphon before giving chase. Circling upwards, Eldon avoided Cynder's deadly flames—but he could not escape the dragon's tail. It struck the gryphon's body, stunning the mighty creature in midair. Eldon crashed to the ground and lay still. Sensing victory, Cynder did not give his enemy a chance to recover. He dove straight down, his cruel claws outstretched. Using his massive weight, the dragon planned to crush the gryphon just as he had done to other beasts countless times before.

The giants, however, had already begun to move. Ollom shouted an order as he and six others quickly formed a ring around the wounded gryphon. Childeric looked on in confusion. Were they going to attack the poor creature? Then the giants knelt down, dug the shafts of their spears into the earth, and pointed the sharp tips upward. Suddenly, everything became clear. Too late Cynder realized he could not stop his momentum. The dragon scorched the giants with his breath as he descended but they raised their shields and avoided the flames.

What happened next would haunt Childeric's dreams for many years. Cynder fell like a lightning bolt, screaming in pain as he impaled himself on seven iron spears, his own strength spelling his doom. Cynder's landing crushed three giants, but the others were able to dive out of the way, including Ollom, as he dragged Eldon to safety a second before the dragon crashed to earth.

Cynder roared again. However, it was clear that the beast was mortally wounded, pierced with spears that not even his scaly armor could turn away. Childeric dared not approach. Instead, he stood with the rest of the giants as the dragon thrashed about, his tail coiling over and over like a wounded snake. The beast tried to rise but collapsed again, broken and exhausted.

Cynder raised his head. "I know you're near, little king," he hissed, casting his baleful eyes this way and that. "I can feel my seed's magic in you—and I can hear your thoughts." Childeric realized the dragon had stopped, and was now looking directly at him. The beast's yellow eyes glowed ominously in the twilight. "Ah," Cynder smiled cruelly. "There you are."

Childeric froze, unable to look away. He was under the dragon's spell.

"You desire a dragon's power?" said Cynder. "Then take it, fool, though you may find wielding it more than you bargained for. May you and your descendants share this power until it destroys you."

Then he laughed. I don't know if you have ever heard a dragon laugh but it isn't pleasant. There is no mirth or joy in it, only malice and mockery. Soon enough, however, the dragon's laugh sputtered into a fit of coughing, the light went out of his great eyes, a last wisp of smoke rose from his nostrils, and Cynder died.

1

A BEAUTIFUL PRISON

Many years later, Childeric's grandson, King Argus, ruled over Valmar in an old, vine-covered castle that straddled the sea's sun-baked cliffs. The castle was called Ballan á Moor and it meant "crown of spears" in the tongue of the Western Giants. They had helped Childeric and his people build a new foundation not far from where the dragon had been killed. That, however, was long ago when giants were still friends with men. Valmar, though still beautiful, had become a more troubled place.

Argus, along with Thelda, Valmar's queen, had two children. Gwendolyn was twelve years old, and Aethelred, her brother, was ten. Despite the difficulties with the giants, what could be more desirable than ruling over a green, wind-swept island with rugged mountains and lush, fertile valleys? What kind of child wouldn't want to live in a many-windowed castle that overlooked the sea?

Gwendolyn, for one. You see, Valmar had become a prison of sorts. Ever since Merovia, the country's stronger southern neighbor, had invaded twelve long years ago, no one had been allowed to leave the island on pain of death. The Valmarians had become a conquered people, a captive people, forced to do the bidding of others.

Led by Sköll, Merovia's cruel king, Valmar had been attacked and overrun shortly before Gwendolyn was born. Her father and the rest of his people had fought bravely, but they were vastly outnumbered. "The masts of their navy were like a forest upon the sea," she remembered her father saying. "We could only watch and wait as their heavy cannons pelted our coastal towns."

After the Merovians had captured Ballan á Moor itself, they plundered the country's wealth but spared the lives of Gwendolyn's parents. This was not done out of kindness. Sköll was a shrewd man. He knew that by killing the island's rulers, he would only stoke a new rebellion that could last for years. The presence of men in the north also kept the Western Giants in check. But he was determined to keep Valmar from growing strong enough to challenge him. Before he left with his army, Sköll decreed that the Valmarians could never again leave the island, save for fishing their coasts. He also demanded an annual tribute, which kept Valmar poor. Perhaps worst of all, the defeat had left Gwendolyn's father a broken man.

That winter, on one of the darkest days of the year, and with Valmar in disarray, Gwendolyn was born. Argus stood outside of the room where his queen lay while the midwife helped with the delivery. He paced back and forth for what seemed like hours, anxiously listening to his wife cry out in pain just a few feet beyond the bedroom door. Soon, Thelda's screaming ceased, and he heard another sound—the shrill cry of an infant. After a few minutes, the midwife opened the door.

"Congratulations, sire," said the old woman. "It's a girl. Very healthy lungs from the sound of her."

Argus entered the room and saw his wife cradling the child. Thelda looked up at him and smiled. He let out a long, slow sigh, and smiled back wearily, not realizing until now that he had been holding his breath. "All is well?" he asked, taking his wife's hand and squeezing it gently.

Thelda smiled more broadly. "All is well," she answered. "Meet your daughter." The queen lifted the swaddled child and he took the girl into his arms. She had black hair, bright blue eyes, and a round nose. Argus smiled down at her. For a moment, the baby stopped crying and looked up at him.

"Do you see that, Thelda?" replied the king. "She's stopped crying. Do you think she recognizes my voice?" As he finished, however, her cries started anew, and were now even louder than before.

"Here," laughed Thelda, taking the baby back into her arms. "She's hungry, that's all."

"Or she cries because she's just realized that she's been born into this world of fools," said the king wryly, as thoughts of Sköll and Merovia darkened his mood.

Thelda ignored his words. "What shall we name her?"

Argus smiled in spite of his thoughts. "Gwendolyn," he said, looking down at the little baby with whom he had already fallen in love. "We'll call her Gwendolyn."

***

As the years passed, Gwendolyn's parents realized that their daughter had an extraordinary amount of courage. For instance, she had never been afraid of the dark. In fact, she preferred to explore the nearby forest alone at dusk, sneaking out of her bedroom to take long walks while learning the ways of the animals that lived there. She delighted in watching the deer graze meekly on grass and clover as the squirrels chattered noisily overhead. She could tell you the difference between a kestrel and a falcon, and why owls are able to fly so silently. Sometimes, she would even glimpse coyotes as they padded silently through the trees, or wild boars as they searched for mushrooms at dawn. In fact, she was not even afraid of approaching the wild horses in the meadow near the castle, carefully holding out her hand to make friends, while they stamped and snorted in the cold morning air. That's not to say she didn't feel fear or recognize danger. She certainly did. Gwendolyn, however, had courage, which is not the absence of fear but rather the mastery of it.

Gwendolyn's brother, Aethelred, was different. Though two years younger than his sister, he was tall for his age with bright red hair, a long, straight nose, and fair skin like his mother. His smile and laughter were infectious, bringing joy into a castle that too often lacked amusement. He was also a good student—sometimes puzzling out a logic problem that would quickly frustrate or bore his sister. Unlike Gwendolyn, though, he was still afraid of the dark.

As they grew older, Gwendolyn took Aethelred with her to explore the island's northern territory. They learned where the narrow parts of the Restless River would freeze during winter, creating a smooth, slippery surface on which to play. They learned how far from shore the fishermen were permitted to go before they might be seen by a Merovian warship patrolling nearby.

They learned where to find the sweetest strawberries in the spring, and why the trunk of an oak tree made for the best spot to take a nap. They were never allowed, however, to go very far from the castle. Wolves still lived in the vast forests and mountain ranges that surrounded Ballan á Moor, as well as other creatures. Predictably, the fact that she had been forbidden to visit such places made Gwendolyn want to explore them all the more.

Was she brave or reckless? Sometimes it was hard to tell the difference. We can forgive Gwendolyn, however, if she took risks. For as she grew older, her heart chafed against the boundaries designed to tame it—and Valmar would need untamed hearts in the days ahead.

***

During the summer, Gwendolyn could sometimes be found playing among the stone ruins of Childeric's Keep, about a mile east of where she lived. It had once been the site of her great-grandfather's castle but the place had been destroyed by Cynder long ago. After the dragon was killed, however, the Western Giants had used it as a stone quarry to help Childeric and his people build Ballan á Moor near the cliffs where they thought a new castle could be better defended. Childeric's Keep was now a solitary place, consisting of a few ruined stone columns that had been overtaken by tall grass, moss, and large tree roots.

Though she wasn't exactly sure why, Gwendolyn felt drawn to this place. The cliffs a short distance from where the ruins stood also provided a good view of the sea. Here she would scan the broad horizon and enjoy the feel of the stiff north wind on her cheeks as she watched the fishing boats return to shore in the evening. The fishermen's weathered hands and faces fascinated her, as did their uneducated speech and, above all, their talk of the sea. Some days, she would loiter along the beach just to hear them converse with one another.

"The sea's a tyrant," she once heard an old sailor say to his young apprentice, as they hauled the day's catch from the ship's hold in the harbor. "At peace one minute, storming the next. You can serve it your whole life, but you must never trust it."

"But we must trust it," thought Gwendolyn, frustrated with the old man's wisdom. "Or, if not trust it, put our lives in its hands nevertheless. Otherwise, we'll remain chained to this island forever."

Thelda found her daughter among the ruins one day watching the seagulls as they floated gracefully on the rising air. The queen was a beautiful woman, tall and proud, but the furrows on her alabaster brow betrayed the years of worry. She loved her husband, and though it grieved her to know that Argus hated paying tribute to a wicked man like Sköll, she also knew that her children would pay with their lives if Valmar revolted. Still, even if the uneasy peace was maintained, she worried what would become of them when she and her husband were gone. So she focused on protecting her husband and children, one day at a time, encouraging them, and loving them as best she knew how.

"You look serious this morning," said the queen, draping a shawl around her shoulders to protect against the wind as she approached her daughter in the tall grass. "What do you look for so intently?"

"Merovian ships," jested Gwendolyn, who was playing with a chunk of broken marble that she had found among the ruins. "Perhaps when I get older, I will be able to sink them." She held up the stone. "I have good aim, you know."

"What would you do if you sank them?" asked her mother, bemused.

Gwendolyn turned and looked at her mother with great seriousness. "Sail day and night until I reached the end of the world."

Thelda sighed. Her daughter often made comments like this but she had to learn to accept the terms of defeat. There was no use stoking thoughts of rebellion. Valmar lacked the numbers to stage a successful revolt. It was that simple. "Have you forgotten that we are forbidden to leave this island?" asked her mother. "Besides, you have everything you could wish for right here. What do you hope to find that is not already in Valmar?"

"That's just it," said Gwendolyn, impatiently. "I don't *know* what else is out there. Aren't you curious, mother?"

"Curiosity is a luxury that only the young, it seems, can afford, my dear," responded Thelda, looking older as she said this, and pulling the shawl more tightly about her. "Your father and I must play the more practical role of governing. And one day, you and your brother must put away childish things and learn how to govern, too."

"Uncle Wulfric doesn't seem to think governing so important," said Gwendolyn, glancing at her mother quickly to see her reaction.

Thelda shook her head in disapproval. "Your uncle and his men act irresponsibly," she scolded. "His actions endanger us all."

Wulfric was the king's younger brother, and of course, Gwendolyn's uncle. Both men had fought bravely together during the invasion but, unlike Gwendolyn's father, Wulfric could never bring himself to accept Merovian rule. He had left mysteriously one night three years ago on a small fishing boat with some loyal followers—and in defiance of Sköll's edict. No one had seen them since.

"I don't blame him," said Gwendolyn defiantly, keeping her eyes fixed on the horizon. "Besides, father governs in name only. If he stopped paying those wretched Merovians, their navy would be back in a matter of weeks. We would all simply be put in a smaller cage."

The queen thought of rebuking her, but she realized that Gwendolyn was just giving voice to what many others felt. Following her gaze out to sea, Thelda stroked her daughter's hair. "Your father has made a great sacrifice. He despises Sköll, but his duty is to protect his people. He could not do that by fleeing our home or risking more death. In time, I hope you can understand that."

Gwendolyn remained silent, and her grip tightened on the marble fragment that she held in her hand. She had no desire to govern—no desire to rule over farming disputes or pay tribute to a foreign king. She wanted only to defeat her enemies when she was grown, and set sail on the open sea. If only she knew how quickly her chance would come.

2

A PECULIAR TREASURE

Do you ever wonder why it seems that magic has disappeared from the world? Why there are no more ogres lurking under bridges, for example, or dragons hovering fatally overhead? Or perhaps most tragically, why heroes seem to be in such short supply?

Gwendolyn did. When would Valmar be delivered from its bondage? There were other ways than war to gain their freedom. Why, for instance, didn't her father simply challenge Sköll to single combat? Was he afraid? She envisioned both kings on opposite ends of a grassy field as a steady rain fell. Her father was mounted high on a warhorse, its flanks covered in scarlet. He lowered his visor confidently, tightened his grip on his lance, dug his heels into his horse's sides, and galloped toward a hesitant Sköll.

Her mind then wandered to another, more familiar scene. There was her father, haggard and unshaven, sitting wearily on his throne, besieged by a thousand mundane worries. He had no visor or lance. No wicked king quailed before him. Rather, King Argus seemed outmatched by an endless stream of parchment that piled around him, awaiting his signature. Every day that he failed to act, failed to pick up his sword and don armor to lead a rebellion, Gwendolyn felt more ashamed for him. For she loved her father dearly, and her love fueled her anger.

These thoughts filled her mind one morning as she sat surrounded by books in her tutor's study, trying to remember her history lesson, a subject she loathed. Her tutor, Polonius, was seated at his desk in front of her. He was an enormous man, extremely tall and more than a little fat. His hands were the size of large hams, and when he sneezed, the entire castle seemed to shake. He wore thick glasses which, along with his large nose, made him look like a giant owl. Although he rarely smiled, Polonius had a sharp mind, a kind heart, and a patient spirit—all of which he needed today. They were discussing the history of the Giant Wars, and Gwendolyn feigned interest while trying not to look out the window.

Her tutor continued, "After the king died of plague in the winter of —"

"Sorry, Polonius," she said, distracted. "Which king was that?"

"Childeric," responded Polonius. "As you'll recall from yesterday's lesson, your great-grandfather was the first king to sign a treaty with the Western Giants when the trolls threatened Valmar."

"I thought Childeric fought the giants," she said, frowning slightly in confusion.

"No, the treaty with the giants wasn't broken until your grandfather, Edubard, sat on the throne," the old man patiently explained. "During Childeric's reign, the giants were friendly with men. In fact, if this castle hadn't been designed and built with their help, it probably would not have later withstood the siege of the troll armies."

"It doesn't look like it was built by giants," said Gwendolyn, skeptically. "If they made it, wouldn't everything be bigger?"

"I said it was designed and built with their help," Polonius reminded her. "The giants assisted in laying the foundation, which is why the stone is so thick. If you remember yesterday's lesson, a dragon had destroyed Childeric's original castle—which was more of a keep."

Unfortunately, Gwendolyn hadn't been paying much attention to yesterday's lesson either. History didn't interest her. That was more of her brother's hobby. She preferred to day dream instead, imagining she was sailing in rough weather and battling pirates. Still, she acted interested for Polonius's sake.

She slouched down in her chair and stifled a yawn. "Who was responsible for breaking the treaty between us and the giants?"

"It depends who you ask, I suppose," said Polonius, sounding very much like a historian. "When the troll armies were finally defeated by men and giants, Childeric was very old. He died from the plague shortly before the war ended, and his son became king."

"Edubard the Giant Killer!" said Gwendolyn, thankful that she could at least remember that.

"Yes, that was one of his names," Polonius responded, sighing. Did he look sad? "But giants and men were not always distrustful of one another. In return for helping him drive the trolls back into the Solitary Marshes and finish the construction of Ballan á Moor, Childeric gave the giants quite a bit of gold."

"I remember that part," said Gwendolyn. "Childeric plundered the dragon's lair after the giants killed the beast, which made him a very wealthy king."

"Correct," he said. "The giants gratefully accepted some of Childeric's gold before he died. However, they also insisted on something else after they had built the castle in which you now sit—something more than gold and jewels."

Gwendolyn sat up, interested. "What did they want?"

"It's a matter of some debate," explained Polonius. "Some historians claim the giants wanted to rule Valmar. Others say they wanted to be paid in children."

Gwendolyn gasped. "In children?"

"To eat," said the old man. "That, however, is almost certainly false. As everyone knows, giants are vegetarians."

"So we don't know who broke the treaty?" she asked.

Polonius took off his glasses and began polishing them on his shirt. "The giants maintain that Edubard broke it by refusing to honor Childeric's original promise."

"What promise?"

"According to the giants, Childeric promised them a peculiar treasure that he had found as a young man."

"What was it?"

Polonius suddenly looked troubled. "There has been much speculation on that subject," he said. He put his glasses back on and turned to the window. "The only thing we are sure of is that shortly after the trolls were defeated, a dispute arose between men and giants. They rejected Edubard's offer of more gold, insisting on the treasure his father had promised them. Childeric died before the matter could be settled. Then, a new war began. Edubard and his men fought the giants for years before finally driving them back to Grimstad. There the giants remain behind their walls high in the Skelding mountains, distrustful of men."

"Oh, to live in such times," exclaimed Gwendolyn, wistfully. "Trolls, Polonius! Giants! It must have been exciting! Just think of it!"

He turned from the window and looked down on her gravely. "Are you thinking of it, Gwendolyn?" he asked. "Carefully? War may be exciting—but it is certainly terrifying. The battle left many dead on both sides. It is a pity that the alliance between men and giants failed."

"I suppose you're right," she admitted reluctantly. "But people these days are always acting so carefully." She thought of her father again as he poured over a sea of parchment while his sword rusted in its sheath.

"Perhaps that's why you're still here," said Polonius with the hint of a smile. "Careful can be good." He walked to his desk and picked up his pipe, filling it with tobacco.

"Yes, but can't one be both careful and brave?" she asked, staring back at him defiantly.

"Indeed, one may," said Polonius thoughtfully. "King Argus, for instance—"

"My father?" she interrupted, losing her patience. "If my father were brave, he would have built a new navy by now and defeated Sköll. Instead we remain little more than slaves."

"Princess," said Polonius softly, shaking his head. "You don't know of what you speak."

"I know only too well! If my father had been more like Uncle Wulfric, we would be free by now."

"That's not fair," he said, with the rare note of anger in his voice. "The king is one of the bravest men I know." His eyes wandered, as if recalling a distant memory. "And what a sailor! He could beat a storm to shore, and finish dinner before the rough waves lapped the sand." Then, he focused on Gwendolyn. "Even great warriors, however, must bide their time."

Gwendolyn was not convinced. "We've waited long enough. I want the chance to sail. I want the chance to fight. What's the use of learning everything you teach me if I don't have the opportunity to put it to use?"

Polonius pursed his lips, and looked out the window.

***

Gwendolyn awoke the next morning to the sound of thunder and hard rain. The curtains to the doors and windows of her private balcony were closed but light still filtered through which told her that it must be a couple of hours past dawn. Suddenly, she heard something outside on the balcony itself—the sound of ceramic breaking against stone. Telling herself that the storm must have blown over one of the many flowerpots she owned, she covered her head with her pillow and tried to fall back asleep. Then she heard another pot break. Rising from her mahogany bed, she pulled aside the window curtains and stifled a scream.

Perched on top of the balcony's stone ledge, a gryphon sat balanced perfectly still in the rain, his wings folded neatly behind him. Fragments of several smashed flower pots lay at his feet. His tail twitched from side to side while his large, muscular frame, covered in red and yellow feathers, stood out brilliantly against the dull, gray sky.

As Gwendolyn stared at the gryphon, she realized he was staring right back at her. The downpour didn't seem to bother the creature one bit. He sat patiently gazing through the window at her, occasionally cocking his head from side to side as the rain beaded off his sleek, feathered head. She remembered that while gryphons were highly intelligent, they were not wicked. What could he want? There was only one way to find out. She took a deep breath and flung the doors open.

"Hail, Gwendolyn of Valmar!" said the gryphon, solemnly.

Gwendolyn didn't quite know how to respond. She had never spoken to a gryphon before. Fortunately, she remembered her manners.

"Hail, friend of men," she replied. She thought he seemed pleased with her words.

"I am Eldon," he declared. "But I come with unfriendly tidings—and we don't have much time."

She stood for a moment, wondering what the news could possibly be—and how the gryphon knew her name. She would have probably stood there several more minutes pondering these questions but the sound of thunder roused her. "I hope your news is not as bad as the weather," she said, looking past the beast at the lightning that flickered in the background. "Please, come inside." She opened the balcony doors wider, and stood back as the gryphon shook the water from his body and walked into her room.

Once inside, she shut the doors while the gryphon turned toward her and folded his wings majestically.

"You've shown better manners—and better sense—than Childeric did when I first met him long ago."

Gwendolyn's heart skipped a beat. "You—you knew my great-grandfather?"

"I should think so," replied Eldon. "It was I who helped establish the alliance between men and giants long ago before the greed of both races destroyed it. I am here because now you must rebuild that friendship."

Gwendolyn looked confused. "I don't understand."

"The Merovian fleet approaches," explained the gryphon, grimly. "It will reach Ballan á Moor in a matter of days. You and your people must make peace with the giants and fight Sköll's army as one. It is your only chance of surviving the invasion."

Gwendolyn was stunned. Why would the Merovians attack when Valmar had faithfully paid tribute all these years? What would Sköll gain by conquering the entire island? Then she thought about what the gryphon had said. They needed the giants to survive. But why would they help now? Twelve years ago, when the Merovians had invaded the northern coast of Valmar, the giants had done nothing as Argus and his people were defeated. Instead, they had simply remained behind the high walls of their mountain castle. Why would they act any differently now that Sköll was back?

"Have you spoken to my father?" she asked, turning to leave. "We must prepare immediately."

"I have already warned him," said Eldon. "I have come here because you must ask the giants for their help."

"Yes, I understand we could use their help, but—"

"No, Gwendolyn," replied the gryphon, firmly. "I said *you* must ask for their help."

"Me?" she asked in disbelief. "Why me?"

"Your father has refused. He cannot conquer his greatest enemy—his fear," said Eldon. "He fears and distrusts the giants. It has hardened his heart. But you! Look at how you have behaved, opening your doors to me without the least hesitation. Now you must find a way to open the door to the giants."

"Why should the giants help us?" continued Gwendolyn. "There hasn't been peace between us for almost a hundred years."

"You must convince them that Sköll's army will not stop at Ballan á Moor this time," he added. "The Merovians mean to march on Grimstad."

"The giant city…" said Gwendolyn, trying to remember her geography lessons.

"Yes," Eldon replied. "The giants are fierce warriors but they are also few. They cannot withstand a siege forever—especially against an army as large as Sköll's."

"What am I to say to them?" she asked.

The gryphon seemed to smile. "It will please them that Valmar's princess and heir of Childeric asks for their help," he responded. "They believe men have grown too proud—and they still believe they are owed something. You must make them understand that unless you stand together you will die alone."

Suddenly, a strange cry could be heard overhead. Eldon and Gwendolyn walked out to the balcony and looked up into the rain. Another gryphon hovered in the storm clouds above. The creature seemed to pause for a moment, looking down at them before streaking away south.

"Khailen calls me." He leaped up to the stone railing and looked back at Gwendolyn. "Will you ask the giants for help?"

Gwendolyn hesitated. She had always been told by her father that the giants had betrayed men, breaking the treaty that was signed so long ago. It was certainly true that they had not helped her people when Sköll's army attacked. But the chance of gaining the giants as allies to defeat Sköll once and for all made sense. She had to try. It certainly sounded like an adventure.

"I will go," she declared. "First, however, I must tell my mother and father."

"I have already tried to persuade your father," said Eldon, frustrated. "He will not understand."

"Nevertheless," she replied, stubbornly. "I must try."

"You remind me of Childeric," said the gryphon, spreading his wings and rising into the air. "Do not be surprised when he forbids you to go. Above all, do not allow fear to rule your heart." Then the gryphon rose into the air.

Gwendolyn watched him fly away into the Skelding mountains. After she had dressed, she hurried down the hallway to her parent's chamber door, which was located on the third and highest story of the castle. She raised her hand to knock but stopped when she heard her father's voice raised in anger.

"Where would we flee, Thelda?" came the king's voice. "No, the castle is the safest place!" Gwendolyn stopped, and pressed her ear against the door to listen. She knew that it wasn't polite to eavesdrop, but her curiosity was too great.

"We cannot remain here indefinitely," said her mother, quietly. "We need the giants' help."

"I will never ask for their help," replied her father, angrily. "Don't you remember? They did nothing while our people were butchered by Sköll's army. What more do we have to say to them?"

"Peace," Gwendolyn heard her mother's soft voice. "The Giant Wars were long and hard. Surely they have reason to distrust us just as we distrust them?"

"Reasons?" thundered Argus. "What reasons? My father offered them gold in return for their help all those years ago. They refused his generosity, however, insisting on some imaginary treasure. Let their pride take them!"

"Pride," said Thelda sadly. "It seems like we have at least that in common with them."

"Do not fight me on this, Thelda!"

"Listen to yourself," the queen explained, impatiently. "We have very little time before the Merovian fleet is floating in our harbor. Perhaps we can make a stand at Grimstad together with the giants. We should send Gwendolyn to ask for their help, as the gryphon advised."

"And risk her life?" scoffed the king. "No! The giants have our people's blood on their hands. If they apologize, I'll listen. I'll not humiliate our family, however, by sending my daughter on a fool's errand."

Eldon was right, thought Gwendolyn. Her father's heart had grown too hard to ask for help. It was no use arguing with him. If her mother couldn't convince him, no one could. Why could he not see that peace with the giants was the only way to survive?

"We must prepare for the siege," declared the king, ending the discussion. "I will tell my knights to make the necessary preparations. We must bring the villagers inside the castle walls before Sköll's men land."

Gwendolyn heard her father's heavy footsteps approach the door. If he was angry now, he'd be furious if he caught her spying on them. She needed to move quickly. There was another door opposite the royal chamber. Her brother's room! She disappeared behind it just in time as her father stepped into the hallway.

"Gwen! Can't you knock!" came Aethelred's sleepy voice. He was still burrowed in his bed furs when she entered, and had only just awakened.

"Shhhh!" whispered Gwendolyn, motioning for him to keep quiet. Aethelred looked annoyed, rubbed his eyes, and sat up on his bed. Her brother was her best friend. The thought of leaving him behind tormented her. If she was going to visit the giants, she decided, he was coming with her.

"What's going on?" asked Aethelred, now fully awake. "Why are we whispering?"

Gwendolyn heard the sound of her father's footsteps diminish as he walked down the hallway. She exhaled and sat down on Aethelred's bed before looking up at him.

"I don't think you're going to believe me when I tell you," she said, her eyes sparkling with excitement. "How would you like to meet the giants?"

3

UNCLE WULFRIC RETURNS

Once they had packed a few items of clothing for their journey, Gwendolyn and Aethelred hurried downstairs and entered the Great Hall. It was a cavernous room, big enough to accommodate all of the king's courtiers and knights-at-arms during happier times when the Valmarians had gathered together for feasts or other special occasions. Long oak tables and benches lined the walls. Two fireplaces, each large enough to burn many logs at once, stood in opposite corners. Narrow, stained-glass windows looked down on them, separated by paintings and tapestries with scenes of famous battles, long-dead relatives, and splendid hunts.

It had been years, however, since Childeric and his people had feasted in the Great Hall. The place stood sterile and empty, more like a mausoleum than a dining room. Thanks to Sköll and his army, many of the same courtiers and knights who had once laughed and sung so merrily under its rafters now lay buried nearby. The memories were too painful for King Argus and he had decreed that it was never to be used again.

Gwendolyn looked up at the portraits of Valmar's kings. There were over a dozen men but the only two she could recognize were her great-grandfather, Childeric, and his son, Edubard. Both kings, dressed in crimson robes and thick animal furs, stared solemnly down upon her. Gwendolyn scolded herself for not paying better attention during her history lessons. Now that she had learned a bit more about her ancestors, the kings seemed different somehow. Not so distant. Almost human. She wondered what secrets they had taken with them to the grave. What would they have done now in her circumstances as Sköll's navy approached? Would they have tried to make peace with the giants as Eldon suggested? Or would they have dug in and tried to resist the Merovians all by themselves?

When she had reached the other end of the Great Hall with her brother, she followed him into a smaller room where the royal family took their breakfast most mornings. It was a modest place, with only a large, wooden table and four chairs. The children sat down quickly and called for breakfast. They did not want to wait for their parents to appear. Instead, they would eat quickly, collect more food for the journey, and sneak out of the castle before heading south into the mountains. Gwendolyn did not know how to reach the stronghold of the giants but she expected the trip to only take a few days. Besides, she thought, if they travelled far enough south, they would have no need of finding Grimstad; the giants would almost certainly find them.

Soon, a servant appeared with plates of hard-boiled eggs, sliced ham, pears, goat's milk, and freshly picked blueberries. Eager to depart, the children filled their bellies with scarcely a word between them. Then they gathered the rest of the food, wrapped it in cloth, and put it in their packs. Just as they were about to leave, however, their mother entered the room, looking worried.

"There you are! I've been looking for you." She sat down opposite them and examined the empty plates. "It seems you've already started without your father and me." The queen pointed at the gear near the children's feet. "Are you going somewhere?"

Gwendolyn refused to lie. "We know about the invasion," she said, standing as she slung the bag over her shoulder. "Aethelred and I are going to ask the giants for help." Her brother stood next to her and nodded in agreement.

Thelda frowned. "Who told you we're being invaded?"

"The gryphon came to my room this morning," explained Gwendolyn.

A deep voice sounded from behind them. "Then he has betrayed me!" The children turned and saw the king standing in the doorway. He had thick, red hair that hung down almost to his shoulders, and his eyes were the color of the sea. In his grip was a sword that hung loosely from his belt. Though Gwendolyn had seen her father in dark moods before, she had never seen him look so fierce nor so somber. She realized that her impression of him as a coward may have been misguided. Still, she recovered her wits in time to answer him.

"Betrayed you?" she asked. "No, father. Eldon is a friend."

"A friend now?" replied her father, raising his eyebrows. "A friend would not put my daughter's life in danger by sending her to beg for a false peace."

"You must see that without help from the giants we won't last a week," she pleaded.

The king shook his head in defiance. "These walls are thick," he responded, putting his hand on the stone archway. "We can last for months with the provisions we are gathering."

"But —"

"You may not leave the castle," he ordered, staring down at the children. "Do I make myself clear?"

Suddenly, a knight ran into the room. Argus motioned him forward and the knight spoke in low tones.

"What? Here?" replied Argus, angrily. "Too little too late, I'm afraid."

Gwendolyn and Aethelred looked at one another. What could make their father so upset? Then they heard a familiar laugh coming from the Great Hall. Only one person had that laugh.

"Uncle Wulfric!" shouted Aethelred, running out of the room. Gwendolyn and her parents followed the boy into the Great Hall and saw that it was indeed Wulfric. He was accompanied by another man, Melko, whom the children recognized as a veteran sailor lucky enough to survive Merovia's attack. No one had seen either man for three years.

Wulfric, grinning from ear to ear, opened his arms wide. "My young warriors!" The children ran to him and he scooped both of them up, laughing, as the king and queen stared in disbelief.

A tall, muscular man with red hair and blue eyes, Wulfric clearly resembled Gwendolyn's father. Despite their physical similarities however, the two men couldn't have been more different. Her father was often distracted by his responsibilities—and rarely in the mood for games. Uncle Wulfric, however, smiled often and enjoyed the children's company. He, too, wore armor but he wore it more easily because he lived in it. Unfortunately, Wulfric and Argus didn't get along. The king thought Wulfric irresponsible while Wulfric thought Argus a bore.

Wulfric set the children down. "Oh, how I've missed you!" he said. "Have they treated you well while I've been gone? Not too much schooling? I should have taken you with me. You would have learned some good lessons at sea—the kind you can't learn from that old crank, Polonius!"

"I'm ready!" replied Aethelred. "I can handle a sword, and would make a Merovian sorry if he chose to fight me!"

The king frowned but Wulfric took no notice. "I'm sure you would, Aethelred," laughed Wulfric. "We'll have need of brave young men like you in the days ahead, I fear."

Then he bowed to the queen. "My lady," he said, smiling. "If there's one thing I have missed while sailing the seas, it's the sight of a beautiful woman."

Thelda nodded her head and returned his smile. "It is good to see you again, Wulfric. I'm glad you haven't lost the art of flattery."

The king scowled. "Perhaps not—but he has certainly lost his mind." Argus stared at his brother with contempt. "You are very bold, sir, returning here after abandoning us. It's been three years since we last saw your face, and you act like you just returned from gathering firewood. I should throw you in the dungeon for threatening the peace." He turned his icy gaze on Melko. "You and all of those who were foolish enough to follow you."

Wulfric simply smiled. "Would you really imprison those in Valmar's navy as the Merovians draw near?"

"Valmar's navy, you say?" snorted the king. "You have one ship. Do you really think you can defend us against the might of Sköll's fleet?"

Wulfric shook his head and smirked. "You're always asking rhetorical questions, Argus. Perhaps that's why you can only see the obvious." Suddenly, he grew serious. "It's not my ship, but my cargo, that may even the odds."

"Come!" replied Argus. "We don't have time for your riddles! Speak plainly!"

"I rescued a Merovian boy in Moska," began Wulfric. "He—"

"In Moska?" interrupted the queen. "Do you mean to say that you have been to Merovia's capital?"

"Indeed," explained Wulfric, with an exaggerated bow. "We just returned. Unfortunately, Sköll never asked us to dinner." He turned to the children and winked. "Such a rude host. Don't you think?" The children giggled but their laughter quickly faded when their father spoke.

"Are you in league with the Merovians?" he thundered.

"Of course not," snapped Wulfric. The king's questions were beginning to anger him but he tried to remain calm. "My men and I have learned to disguise ourselves and our ship as a foreign trading vessel from the east. But underneath our disguises, I assure you we remain free men of Valmar." He looked at his brother disdainfully. "I wish I could say the same for everyone."

"Free men, you say?" Argus glowered at his brother. "Free to do what? Abandon us so that you can spend time drinking wine in Merovia?"

Wulfric flushed red and gripped his sword hilt. Gwendolyn realized that her uncle shared her father's temper but had done a better job to conceal it—until now. "That's the second time you have questioned my allegiance," said Wulfric quietly. "Do not do so again." The king stared back at Wulfric, stone-faced. He was about to respond but Thelda stepped between them, holding up her hands.

"That's enough!" she cried. "We're wasting precious time. Will you continue to argue until we see Merovian ships in our harbor?" She turned to Wulfric. "You talked about carrying a cargo that may even the odds. What do you mean?"

"I'm sorry, my queen." Wulfric took a deep breath and released the hilt of his sword. "I found a boy in Merovia. His name is Ghael and he tells a tale worth hearing."

"You may not have noticed, Wulfric, but we are preparing for battle," declared Argus, impatiently. "I don't have time for children's tales."

"He claims to be Sköll's nephew—and heir to the Merovian throne," replied Wulfric. "Perhaps that will change your mind?"

"Sköll's nephew?" asked the king, still skeptical. "A Merovian spy more likely."

"Then why would he warn me of the invasion?" explained Wulfric. "Our return here is no coincidence." He looked at Melko and nodded before turning back to Argus. "My men and I will defend Valmar with our lives.

If this boy could command the loyalty of Merovia's navy, however, then perhaps that won't be necessary."

The king frowned. "Very well. I will judge this matter for myself."

"Of course," replied Wulfric. "He is waiting to speak with you." He looked down at the children. "I am sorry that this business must deprive me of your most excellent company, little ones, but I promise I will see you both soon." He bowed gracefully and away.

***

When Valmar had first been conquered, Wulfric was miserable. He was not a fisherman or a blacksmith or a farmer. He was not even a good nobleman, for he treated the peasant-farmers on his land much too fairly. He was a soldier and a sailor—and excellent at both occupations. Nevertheless, after he was defeated in battle by the Merovian navy, Wulfric had tried to govern as his brother did, toiling alongside the people he dearly loved so that they could pay Sköll's high taxes.

The memory of his defeat, however, continued to haunt him. Wulfric could not bear to live on an island that paid tribute to a man like Sköll. He also knew that the Valmarians would never throw off the chains of Sköll's tyranny without someone to lead them to victory. Unfortunately, Argus seemed to have accepted his fate. After nine years of trying to convince his brother to revolt, Wulfric realized it was useless. The king would rather live in peace—even an unjust peace—than risk another war.

One night, Wulfric and a dozen like-minded knights set sail and did not return. Though it broke his heart to leave the home he loved, he vowed to remain at sea until he could find a way to free his people. That meant raising enough money to pay for an army. So Wulfric and his men became pirates—and they were good at it. They grew rich by harassing and plundering Merovian trading ships. Soon, they had enough money to buy a warship from the people of Quintharia, a land far to the east. But that was not all. Wulfric and his men also disguised themselves as humble eastern merchants when necessary, boldly sailing into Merovian ports to sell their wares.

Masquerading as just such a ship, they docked in Merovia's capital port city of Moska for almost a week. As his men loaded the ship with food and provisions during that time, Wulfric noticed that the harbor was unusually full—and not just with other merchant ships. Many of Merovia's warships were assembled as well. Wulfric counted about forty in all—more than Sköll had used to invade Valmar twelve years ago. "I wonder what that navy would do to us if they realized that the pirate ship that had plundered so many of their vessels was docked in their very midst!" he chuckled to himself. "Still, what are they up to?"

On the day they had planned to leave Moska, Wulfric noticed a Merovian boy with black hair and olive skin stopping some of the sailors on the dock and trying to engage them in conversation. His clothes must have been expensive once upon a time but now they were torn and dirty. The boy also looked unnaturally thin. Wulfric suspected he hadn't eaten in a while. The sailors, however, paid him no attention though he pleaded with them.

"Go home," a Merovian sailor from another ship told the boy. "The harbor is no place for beggars."

"Get out of my way," barked another. "Or I'll feed you to the sharks."

The sailors all laughed at these taunts but the boy did not give up. Then, to Wulfric's dismay, the gaunt figure approached his ship. Wulfric did not like to talk to too many people when in Moska. His disguise was convincing, he knew, and would not draw attention but his accent was less certain. He could not afford the least suspicion—especially on a day when the harbor was filled with enemy warships. He quickly drew his hood over his head, shrouding his face in darkness, as the boy stopped in front of him.

"Good day, sir," said the boy, bowing slightly.

"What is it?" asked Wulfric gruffly.

"I wish to accompany you and your crew when you set sail," explained the boy. Now that Wulfric could see him more clearly, he realized that the boy's eyes seemed different from others his age—older somehow, as if they had seen too much. Wulfric had seen plenty of suffering himself. Perhaps the boy had suffered, too? Still, he was not in the business of helping runaways, especially Merovian runaways.

"My ship is not a toy," Wulfric replied, incredulous. "Go home. Your parents are probably wondering where you are."

The boy shook his head. "I am an orphan—and I want to become a sailor," he demanded. "I can even pay you to teach me." He reached into his pocket and pulled out a handful of gold coins.

Wulfric became suspicious. If the boy was an orphan, how had he come by so much gold? In any case, he took a great risk by offering his money to strangers on the docks. Half of the sailors the boy met would have had no problem robbing him before throwing him overboard once at sea. "What is your name?"

"Ghael," came the boy's reply. "I'm a hard worker—let me prove it to you. I'll start by scrubbing the decks if you like."

"I'm sorry, Ghael," said Wulfric, shaking his head. "I don't need another sailor—especially one who doesn't tell the truth. You're not an orphan. Your coins and fine clothes tell me that much."

Ghael colored slightly and raised his chin. "I tell you no lies, sir." Then he dropped his voice to a whisper. "I am indeed an orphan—and my life is in danger."

Wulfric shrugged. "Why should that concern me?" It pained him to say this for he was a good man but he could not be responsible for a Merovian child on his ship. He saw that his men were finishing loading the last of the supplies; they would be ready to leave soon.

Ghael looked desperate. "You must help me!" he begged. "I have nowhere else to go—and Sköll wants me dead."

Now it was Wulfric's turn to grow nervous. He didn't want to attract unwanted attention. A ship's captain having a longer-than-necessary conversation with a boy, especially if it involved Sköll, could look suspicious. "Why would he threaten your life?" Wulfric whispered, looking around warily.

"My mother was the king's sister," replied Ghael.

Wulfric frowned. "Was?"

"My parents died from the plague when I was young."

"I'm sorry," said Wulfric. He thought of Gwendolyn and Aethelred. Though they were not orphans, they were about the same age as this boy. Wouldn't he want someone to help them if their lives were in danger? "Why does Sköll want you dead?"

"I am heir to the Merovian throne—at least for a little while longer," replied Ghael, lowering his eyes. "My uncle means to marry a woman from the southern part of Merovia. As you may know, this has divided the country, for most of the people of Moska still distrust the southerners, believing many of them to be witches and sorcerers."

Wulfric studied the boy from the recesses of his dark hood. "If this woman has a son then you become expendable—is that it?"

Ghael nodded. "Already, there are rumors of a civil war," he replied. "Some in Merovia's fleet are prepared to fight for me and declare me the new king."

This changed things. If Wulfric helped Ghael now, the boy would look upon the Valmarians as friends in a dangerous hour. Perhaps he would even grant them independence again. Had he really found a legitimate heir to Sköll's throne? Something, however, still didn't make sense.

"Why not ask your friends to defend you—hide you if necessary?" asked Wulfric. "Why ask me?"

"Sköll's spies are everywhere—and I don't know who to trust," said Ghael. "I just need to escape until I can form a plan."

Melko shouted from the quarterdeck above them. "The supplies are stored, captain, and the tide is coming in. Shall we raise anchor?"

Wulfric nodded up at his first officer. Then, studying the boy, he pulled on his lower lip, something he always did when deep in thought. "Come," he said, making up his mind. "I may be a fool but you may sail with us."

The boy grinned, relieved. "You will not regret this!"

"See to it that I don't," Wulfric said, looking sternly at his new passenger. In a moment, the ship slowly pulled away from the dock and set sail for the open sea.

***

After Ghael had been given something to eat and drink, Wulfric continued to question the boy in his cabin. He thought that it would make the crew nervous to allow a Merovian boy on board and he was right. Wulfric's men regarded Ghael with suspicion, casting sideway glances and muttering under their breath as he led the boy below deck. Nor did they appreciate the fact that they were to remain disguised as eastern traders—even now that they were safely at sea—until Wulfric discovered more about the boy's true identity. Despite their anxiety, however, they still trusted Wulfric. The captain must have had good reasons to take the boy with them. They would just have to be patient until they knew what those reasons were.

As Wulfric watched Ghael finish a cup of ale, he wondered how long it would take the boy to guess that he and his crew were really from Valmar—and that they had been harassing Merovia's ships for three years. What would Ghael say to that—assuming he was really Sköll's nephew? The boy's words on the dock suggested he had been educated; no street beggar spoke in such a way. Could he really be telling the truth? Wulfric thought about the gold coins that Ghael had offered him so freely a short while ago. If he were a peasant, such an amount would have taken years to earn. Would he really give it away so recklessly? Stranger still, Ghael was completely at the mercy of Wulfric and his crew. If he planned to betray them, he was taking a terrible risk. However, the boy's description of Sköll—the detail of the Merovian king's pride and ruthlessness—was what really convinced Wulfric that the boy was the tyrant's nephew. Only someone with first-hand knowledge of Sköll's ways would know such things. Still, Wulfric continued to ask the boy questions to learn as much as he could.

"You mentioned that there are those in Merovia's fleet willing to support you if it came to war?" asked Wulfric, pouring himself a cup of red wine and staring at the boy from across the table.

"Yes," replied Ghael, pushing his mug away. "Admiral Bane, who controls half the fleet, has pledged allegiance to me. He also said there are even more willing to fight on my behalf if my uncle goes through with the marriage."

This answer pleased Wulfric. "Well, perhaps we can hide you in Valmar. I happen to know someone there who might be able to help you." He still didn't want to reveal his true identity to Ghael but he thought Valmar the safest place for the boy as he sorted out friend from foe. What the boy said next, however, caught him by surprise.

Ghael grinned. "I imagine you do."

"What does that mean?" asked Wulfric, frowning slightly.

"You are Valmarian, are you not?"

Wulfric couldn't hide his agitation. "Why do you say that?"

He and his men were always careful to disguise the ship and themselves by making small changes to the vessel's appearance and by dressing like sailors from foreign lands. Sometimes they wore long, billowy clothes and large turbans that hid their faces and weapons. Other times wool cloaks and heavy boots would suffice. However, they never used the same costume twice when plundering a Merovian trader since those from whom they stole were sure to describe their appearance to Sköll's navy. Of course, they never dressed in their native Valmarian garb. That's why it shocked Wulfric that a young boy could so easily guess his secret. Perhaps Ghael was not as helpless as he first appeared.

"Come!" continued Ghael. "I mean you no harm. You must remember, I *am* Merovian. Surely it is no secret that our navy has been looking for certain pirates for some time?"

"We are not pirates," lied Wulfric. "We come from the east."

"That's fortunate, then," replied Ghael, looking around the cabin. "For I've been in the presence of my uncle several times when he has vowed to do very nasty things to these pirates when he catches them."

Wulfric's eyes narrowed. He didn't like being toyed with. Grabbing the boy, he pushed him against the wall of the cabin. "How do you know this?" he demanded, keeping his voice low. If the crew heard him, they would demand that the boy be thrown overboard immediately.

"I'm sorry!" stammered Ghael. "I recognized your accent. My uncle has suspected for months that the pirate ship that has caused him so much frustration was Valmarian, for none are better sailors. Since your people are not allowed off the island, I guessed that you must be the pirates he seeks!"

"This one is clever," thought Wulfric. "He'll make a good king—if he survives long enough." He relaxed, letting Ghael go, and sat down wearily in his chair. Wulfric shuddered at the thought of what Sköll would do to the Valmarians if he learned that the king's brother was behind his piracies.

"There is another reason I wanted to travel with you," said Ghael, as if guessing Wulfric's thoughts. "I am not the only one in danger."

Wulfric looked up guardedly. "What do you mean?"

"Before I fled my uncle's court, I learned that he is planning to attack the kingdom of Valmar."

"That's ridiculous!" Wulfric objected. "He's already conquered us! Argus pays a handsome tribute! Why would he invade now?" He realized too late that he had revealed the truth of his origins. There was, however, a larger concern. Wulfric remembered the number of warships in the capital city's harbor. Ghael's story sounded true enough. Sköll would only assemble his navy if he was preparing to attack.

"I fear Sköll is no longer interested in Valmar's tribute," said Ghael. "I heard him speaking to his councilors shortly before I fled. He thinks he can make more money by cutting down your forests, damming your rivers, and mining your mountains for gold. The fleet sets sail in a few days."

Wulfric was furious. "Why didn't you tell me this before?"

The boy looked down, ashamed. "I wanted to make sure you took me with you," he replied, meekly. "If I had told you on the dock, you might have left me behind."

"Maybe I'll leave you behind right here in the middle of the sea!" he shouted.

"Please," said the boy. "I only want peace with Valmar. If we can get word to Bane and others loyal to me, we may be able to defeat my uncle's forces before they even reach Valmar."

Wulfric took a deep breath. He shouldn't have lost his temper with this boy. Perhaps there was still hope. "We must hurry back to Valmar," he said. "We must warn the king."

He began pacing back and forth in the cabin. Would King Argus urge his people to fight? Even if they would fight, how would Wulfric raise an army in days? He and his crew had amassed a good amount of gold, but they needed time to recruit soldiers from other lands. Many of Valmar's best fighters had been killed twelve years ago, and not many knights and men-at-arms remained. The majority were farmers and tradesmen who had never been trained to use a sword or a bow. What chance would they have?

"Are you certain he means to attack?" asked Wulfric.

"I heard him give the order myself," promised Ghael.

Wulfric stared back at him, stone-faced. "Then there is no time. We must mount a defense." He opened the cabin door and summoned the sailor outside. "Send the word up to Melko! We return to Valmar! Unfurl every sail we've got! We must reach Ballan á Moor before the Merovians do!"

4

A CONVERSATION INTERRUPTED

Gwendolyn and Aethelred stood in the Great Hall and wondered what the arrival of this mysterious visitor meant to Valmar's future. Could he really avert another war? The gryphon seemed to think such a conflict was inevitable. Gwendolyn's thoughts turned to Eldon and his mate. Where had they gone? Why had they left so abruptly? More importantly, how would she ever reach the giants without disobeying her father? She thought of her tutor. Polonius would know what to do. Her father had made it clear that she was not to leave the castle—but he had not forbidden her from visiting her tutor.

Gwendolyn turned to her brother. "Come on," she said. "I have an idea."

A few moments later they stood in the castle's main courtyard and wondered at the frenzy of activity surrounding them. The square was filled with Valmar's knights, men-at-arms, laborers, and tradesman running this way and that in the rain as they prepared for the Merovian siege. Beyond them, Gwendolyn could see blacksmiths sharpening dull swords, stone masons examining the inner walls, and farmers driving cartloads of precious grain to store in the castle's granary. Still farther away, hundreds of villagers streamed in from the town below along muddy lanes to take refuge behind the castle's stone walls. A pilgrimage of haycarts, horses, sheep, goats, cows, and even a few oxen cluttered the road, making it difficult to see into the fields beyond. The children looked up and saw archers, their faces lined with fear, placing barrels of arrows along the ramparts in preparation for the battle.

"Do you think the gryphons will return before the Merovians arrive?" asked Aethelred, disappointed. "I had hoped to see them."

"I don't know," replied Gwendolyn. She shielded her face from the rain as she examined the skies. "We can either stand here until we are soaking wet or we can ask Polonius what he knows."

Dodging the livestock and wagonwheels that clattered along the cobblestones, the children made their way across the courtyard and finally arrived at Polonius's door. His study, while small, had the luxury of three small windows that faced northeast—which gave him an excellent view of the sea. They knocked and a deep and familiar voice said "Come in!" Gwendolyn opened the door and saw Polonius standing in front of his desk, lost in a book. She loved her tutor's room because it had shelves and shelves of books. Even better, he sometimes allowed her to borrow certain volumes, and she would spend hours in front of the fire reading about distant lands.

He looked up, surprised. "Good morning," he said. "Shouldn't you be with your parents?"

Ignoring his questions, both children started to speak at once. "Have you seen the gryphons this morning, Polonius?" asked Gwendolyn, excitedly.

Aethelred stepped in front of her. "Have you met the Merovian who has returned with Uncle Wulfric?"

The old man held up a hand until they were silent. Then he calmly placed the book back on the shelf before answering them. "No, I have not seen any gryphons this morning," he responded. "As for your uncle, I spoke to him and his young guest early this morning. Wulfric wanted my advice on something—and I gave it to him." The old man gazed out the window, lost in his own thoughts.

"Well?" Gwendolyn folded her arms. "What did he ask?"

Polonius lit his pipe and took a few quick puffs while he looked through one of the small windows that faced the sea. "He wanted to know what I thought of Ghael's claim to the throne."

"Do you think he can really help us?"

The old man looked at her doubtfully. "I simply don't know, my dear. He is certainly familiar with Merovia's affairs for one so young." He gazed through the window once again. "He is also very curious; he asked us as many questions as we asked him."

"Such as?"

"He was interested in how many men we had who could wield a sword or a bow. The strength of our castle walls —"

"That's understandable," said Aethelred. "If Sköll's men catch him, his life will be forfeit. He probably wants to know what chances he has of surviving here."

"Indeed," replied the old man, puffing his pipe. "However, he also asked about the castle's foundations. He seemed to know more about the history of Ballan á Moor than I do."

"That's hard to believe," exclaimed Aethelred. "I thought you knew everything."

"Certainly not," said Polonius, frowning. "But if the boy is who he claims to be, we may have found . . . ." His voice trailed off as he looked out the window. The old man's eyes widened in fright as he dropped his pipe.

"Found what, Polonius?" asked Gwendolyn.

Her tutor looked pale and took a step backward. "Get down!"

The next instant, Gwendolyn heard a sound unlike anything she had ever heard before. It was a savage roar that shook her very bones. An instant later, cries could be heard from the ramparts and surrounding town. Suddenly, an explosion rocked the castle. Then another. Polonius and the children fell to the floor as the books tumbled on top of them.

Things moved very quickly after that. The children could smell smoke and sulphur in the air as the walls shook and cracked. Before they could utter a word, Polonius scrambled to his feet and swept aside his oak desk like it was a toy. The next moment, he pulled up the large rug on which it sat, revealing a trap door underneath.

Gwendolyn stared in wonder. A trap door? Why had she never known about that? But there was no time to think. A third explosion shook the room, sending Aethelred flying through the air where he hit the fireplace and lay still. A second later, an avalanche of stone fell towards him as part of the ceiling above him collapsed. "No!" Gwendolyn screamed, reaching her hands up as if to stop it.

She felt a strange and powerful sensation flow through her body. It was if her desire to protect her brother had kindled an intense heat in her chest, spilling down her arms into her hands and fingers as she continued to scream. The next moment, the stones above her brother's head burst into small pebbles, harmlessly scattering about him. Though Aethelred remained still, he had not been crushed. Gwendolyn sighed and looked at her tutor. He stared back at her in amazement.

Then she heard another roar. This time, however, it was deafening, as if its source was between her ears. She looked up through the hole in the ceiling and saw something she could not immediately comprehend. Two great wings blotted out the light followed by the swish of a massive tail, which brought with it a horrible stench. Overwhelmed by the noise, Gwendolyn dimly saw her tutor yelling and motioning to her. Unfortunately, she couldn't understand him. Every instinct urged her to run but she would not abandon her brother. The dark wings rose up again and she saw the beast's great head thrust itself towards her.

A dragon's head.

More like a skull than a head, the dragon's red snout curled into a cruel smile revealing long, sharp teeth the size of daggers. The muscles in her neck rippled underneath the scales of her armor. Then Gwendolyn looked into her eyes. They were like two giant orbs of liquid fire—and terrible to behold. Gwendolyn went limp and fell to the floor. The dragon rose above her for a moment and she became lost in the beast's pitiless gaze, unable to move, mesmerized by the dragon's spell.

"Hello, little thief." The beast's fiery eyes danced in cruel delight as she watched Gwendolyn but her mouth didn't move save for her savage grin. Somehow,

Gwendolyn could hear the dragon's words but they weren't audible. "I've been searching for you," the beast hissed. "You're going to help me—help me find what was stolen from me."

Then Gwendolyn heard something that sounded like an eagle's cry. The dragon turned her head, causing more of the wall to crumble. Gwendolyn's mind was once again her own. Abruptly, the beast let out a roar and was gone, climbing high into the air. As soon as she departed, the room began to collapse, no longer supported by her great frame. Gwendolyn tried to get up and run to her brother. If she could shield him from the falling stones, he might be able to survive. Instead she felt strong hands lift her and then she was falling, falling, falling into darkness.

***

"Do you hear me?"

Slowly, Gwendolyn opened her eyes but she saw only darkness. Had she gone blind? Her head ached terribly and she felt a cold stone floor beneath her body. The room slowly came into focus. Polonius's face swam above her.

"Can you hear me?" he asked again. Gwendolyn nodded and looked around. It was a small room—or rather a tunnel. A dark tunnel. Somewhere nearby, a torch weakly illuminated Polonius's haggard face. He was holding her head in his lap, and saw the confusion in her eyes.

"Take your time," he whispered gently. "You've been unconscious."

She remembered the dragon's roar and those terrible eyes. She tried to get up but Polonius held her fast. "No, Gwendolyn," he said, reassuringly. "We're safe here for the moment. Rest."

Though she was still scared, the fact that she could no longer see or hear the dragon, coupled with Polonius's soothing voice, allowed her to relax a bit. Had it all been a dream? The dragon's head was something out of a nightmare. She could still remember the beast's horrible smell, her gleaming red scales, and the cruel claws that seemed beyond all comprehension. Then she remembered her brother.

"Where are we, Polonius?" she demanded. "Where's Aethelred?"

"Still above ground," he replied. He looked away, unwilling to meet her gaze. "I couldn't reach him before the walls collapsed . . . I'm sorry."

"What do you mean he's above ground?" she asked, bewildered. "We're not in the castle?"

"We're in a passageway directly below the castle," explained the old man. "When the dragon flew away, the walls around us collapsed. I managed to open the hatch in the floor and pull you down here before we were crushed."

Now that her eyes had grown accustomed to the torch light, she saw stone walls with large wooden beams fixed across the top. The walls had strange symbols on them— some sort of language that she had never seen before. The carvings, however, were very clear. Painted images of giants and men were all around her. She wanted to ask what they were, but the thought of her brother lying helpless above them outweighed her curiosity.

"We must try to find Aethelred," she said, firmly.

"It's impossible to go back up that way," replied her tutor. "I have tried. The opening is buried under tons of stone. Fortunately, there are other ways to the surface."

She noticed that Polonius's face was bleeding. "You're hurt," she said, instinctively reaching up to touch his wound.

"It's nothing," he said. "It could have been much worse for both of us—and for your brother." Then he looked at her intently. "How did you do that?"

Gwendolyn sat up weakly. "Do what?"

"Make the stones explode," stated Polonius. "They were falling on him—on Aethelred—and you turned them into a thousand pieces."

"That's impossible," she replied. "They just missed him."

Polonius shook his head slowly. "No, Gwendolyn. You saved his life."

She remembered the heat that had filled her body when she saw her brother in trouble. She had acted without thinking, screaming in fear and anger as she reached out to him. Did she really cause the stones to explode? Then she remembered the dragon's eyes again, and the beast's noxious breath. Tears ran down her face. "Am I dreaming Polonius?"

He looked into the darkness beyond. "I wish we both were, princess."

"That was a dragon, then?" she asked. "I've never seen one before. I've only read about them in books."

He sighed. "Yes, that was a dragon."

"She seemed to look into my soul," recalled Gwendolyn, shuddering as she remembered the beast's horrible grin. "Her voice was so evil."

"Her *voice*?" Polonius looked confused. "The dragon never spoke."

"Of course she did," Gwendolyn exclaimed. "She told me I was going to help her find something."

The old man watched her curiously. "Indeed? Did *she* say anything else?"

"No," replied Gwendolyn, reaching up and rubbing her head. "I must have fallen after that."

Polonius remained silent, studying her. "Could it be?" he whispered.

Gwendolyn turned to him. "What did you say?"

"I said thank goodness for the gryphons." Polonius stroked her face and smiled. "If it weren't for them, we never could have escaped."

Her eyes widened. "The gryphons? Were those the creatures that I heard?" She remembered the high-pitched scream that had distracted the dragon just before the walls had collapsed.

"Yes," he said. "They seemed to come from nowhere. I'll wager the dragon wasn't ready for them."

Gwendolyn looked worried. "What if she's still up there?"

"We're safe here," replied Polonius. "The stone above us is at least ten feet thick. Not even a dragon can get through that. I'm just sorry you hit your head when you fell through the hatch."

She stood up. "I'm fine." Though her head still ached, she had experienced worse landings from falling out of trees. She recalled again Aethelred and the rest of her family. Were they safe? They must reach the surface and find them. "You said there are other ways out of here?"

"Yes," explained Polonius. He took the torch from the wall and pointed down the tunnel. "That way leads west towards the stables. We can emerge there."

Though Gwendolyn and Aethelred had explored every inch of the castle, it had never occurred to them that it might be interconnected by underground passageways. Now she realized that Polonius must have used these tunnels before. "How did you know about this place?"

"The town gates are not the only ways in and out of Ballan á Moor," he added, mysteriously. "Can you walk?"

Though she still felt dizzy, she was determined to find her family. "Yes, I feel fine."

Polonius motioned her forward with the torch. "Then come along."

With Polonius guiding the way, Gwendolyn realized that this was not just a simple tunnel. Rather, it was a maze. Her old tutor led her through a series of complicated passages, twisting and turning again and again until she lost count of the number of corners they had rounded. She would have been hopelessly lost without him. Where did all of these tunnels lead? And how did he know his way so well?

They eventually found a door built into one of the tunnel walls. Polonius stopped and handed Gwendolyn the torch. Then he put his shoulder against the door and pushed. Slowly, it opened and the torchlight revealed a circular staircase inside. Gwendolyn noticed that the walls were no longer made of dirt but of stone. Taking the torch back, Polonius led the way up the stairs and stopped abruptly when they reached a dead end.

She looked around, confused. "What now?"

Ignoring her, Polonius held up the torch and studied the tiled ceiling. Then, reaching up, he found a brass handle and pushed. One of the tiles swung upwards and light streamed into the passageway. "Here we are," he grunted.

A bit dusty, they emerged from the hay-covered floor in the royal stables. It was very quiet. Too quiet. Where were the horses and the grooms? The eerie stillness was broken by human cries in the distance.

Gwendolyn climbed out of the hole, ran to the stable door, and looked out. It had stopped raining. The dragon and the gryphons were nowhere to be seen but the castle's inner walls made it difficult to scan the entire village that surrounded Ballan á Moor. They cautiously crept out into the courtyard for a better view, and were horrified by the scale of the damage.

The front of the castle was in ruins, its proud masonry now just a heap of rubble. Worse, the bodies of dead animals lay strewn across the courtyard, and with them, the broken bodies of Valmarian villagers. Parts of the town below were still on fire. Wooden debris lay scattered everywhere, still smoldering in some places. Dozens of survivors slowly picked through the rubble, helping to free those still half-buried—and to retrieve the dead.

Then there was the dragon stench. It made Gwendolyn's head swim, and she was thankful when she felt Polonius's steady hand on her shoulder.

"The day of reckoning has come," he whispered.

5

FRIENDS IN HIGH PLACES

The dragon's name was Destiny, and she had murder in her eyes.

She was large even for a fully mature dragon. Her wings, mottled red and black, spanned almost one hundred feet from tip to tip, and they were barbed with curved spikes. Her red scales shone like rubies in the sun and she twitched her great tail as she tore through the morning sky.

After hibernating in the Skelding mountains for nearly a century, she had come to reclaim her seed. (A female dragon's egg or "seed" consumes much of its mother's magical power when it's being formed, leaving her weak and vulnerable. In the decades it took to recover, females would often entrust the protection of these seeds to the father.) Upon awakening from her ancient slumber, Destiny had returned to rejoin Cynder in the Valmarian foothills—but she found the place abandoned. Both he and the seed were nowhere to be found. The treasure that they had so painstakingly collected was also gone. Since male dragons only leave their lairs for short periods of time to hunt, it could only mean one thing. Cynder had been killed.

The lair had clearly been deserted for decades for she could no longer pick up a scent. Of course, that would not stop her from taking revenge and recovering what was hers. But who had killed her mate? Who had been foolish enough to take her seed? The trolls? Those cockroaches were always digging holes. Perhaps they had stumbled across the lair and taken her egg back to the heart of a mountain. The thought was almost more than she could bear. If true, there was no way she could reach it. The trolls, however, normally did not come this far north. Could the giants have killed her mate? The giants were fierce adversaries, and though it was difficult to imagine that even the stoutest of them could have pierced a dragon's hide, they could be dangerous in large numbers. She had flown past Grimstad after awakening, however, and had not sensed her seed.

Then her thoughts turned to men. She had not forgotten *them*. Dragons hated men most of all—hated their cunning, their intelligence, and their ambition. Perhaps dragons also hated men because they knew that, like them, men desired gold above all creatures, and would fight to keep it. Destiny had destroyed many kingdoms in her time. She had swallowed more men, women, and children than she could count. If men proved to be responsible for the disappearance of her mate and her seed, her revenge would be terrible indeed.

She searched the island of Valmar for weeks, scanning the forests, the mountains, the deserts, the swamps, and the coastline. She flew low and unseen through the night and morning mists for she did not want to give whatever had killed her mate time to prepare for her wrath. She knew that she would sense her seed's magic if she drew near enough to it. But she had to be patient—and when one lives for centuries, one can afford to be so.

However, despite her best efforts, Destiny found no sign of her seed. She was about to admit defeat and abandon her search when she decided to inspect the island's northern coast for the last time. As she crossed over the Skelding mountains and descended toward the foothills, she suddenly sensed something odd. She smelled the merest hint of her seed's magic on the wind. Picking up speed but still taking care to remain unseen, she flew toward the northern cliffs where the land met the sea. Then her eyes fell upon a great castle—Ballan á Moor. She breathed in deeply through her nostrils. Yes. There could be no mistake. Her seed's magic was near. But while the scent should have been strong and unmistakable, she sensed the magic had become diluted somehow, as if her seed was not whole. No matter. Her heart leaped in her chest. She had found the seed. She would soon be reunited with her child.

The time for stealth was over. She descended from the clouds and attacked Ballan á Moor, ripping it apart stone by stone and beam by beam, delighting in its destruction. She did not, however, destroy recklessly. She remained patient, smelling the air for her seed's power—and tearing down walls that separated her from it. Only when she was sure her egg was safe would she wipe the castle and surrounding village from the earth. She would show no mercy. But where was it?

The scent seemed to be strongest on the first floor of the castle, near the cliffs. When she had torn down the walls to the study, she found no egg. Instead, she saw a large man, accompanied by a boy and girl. They all stood there open-mouthed looking up in terror as so many had before they died. Still, something about the girl gave Destiny pause. She had a strong, red aura. Dragons can see the auras—or the soul's atmosphere—of all living things. Based on the aura's strength and color, dragons can tell if a creature is weak or sickly, or in Gwendolyn's case, remarkably brave and strong. Only magical creatures like gryphons and dragons, however, have red auras. Gwendolyn, whose aura glowed a brilliant red, was clearly neither. There were only two ways a human could share such a color with magical beasts. One was by touching a dragon seed. The other was by inheriting the power from one who had. So this was why the power she sensed was diluted!

Destiny inhaled sharply and was about to send a fireball down upon the girl, turning her into a pile of ash. Then she stopped herself. The girl had her seed's magic flowing in her veins. To Destiny's disgust, the two were connected. The magic that Gwendolyn carried within her must not be destroyed, but restored to the seed. In order to hatch, her child must first be made whole again.

The dragon rammed her head and chest through the stone wall to get a better look at the girl. The force of her entrance sent stones tumbling down into the room. Then something strange happened. The girl screamed and the stones exploded over the boy's head, sparing his life. That type of power could only mean one thing. The girl had indeed inherited her seed's magic. But where was her child? She called out to him using her mind. "I'm here, my beloved," she said. "I'm coming for you." She felt the spirit of her seed respond. It was near. So near she could feel it throbbing in her bones. But where? Buried somewhere? The louder the girl screamed, the closer it felt. "Soon, my love," thought Destiny. "Soon I will find you and restore what is rightfully yours."

Then, as she started to take control of the girl's mind to discover her seed's whereabouts, something surprised Destiny—and she hated surprises. She heard a gryphon's cry and felt the beast land on her back. Destiny tried to turn her head to defend herself but part of the room's stone walls had fallen against her body, making it difficult to move. Then she roared in pain as she felt the gryphon tearing at her scales. Dragon scales are harder than shields but they can be pried loose with great effort. Without her armor, she knew she would forever be vulnerable. Forgetting Gwendolyn for the moment, Destiny rose into the air with terrifying speed, throwing the gryphon backwards.

Spreading his wings, the gryphon righted himself and plummeted past the cliffs toward the beach below. Destiny gave chase, stretching her long serpentine neck so that she could get as close as possible to her prey before blasting the gryphon with a fireball. With a few beats of her powerful wings she overtook Eldon. "Now I have you!" she snarled. She inhaled and felt the familiar sensation of a fireball form in her throat. The beast would be dead in seconds. As she opened her mouth to release the flame, she felt a sharp pain below her chin.

Another gryphon had her by the throat. Where had it come from? Instinctively, she choked and felt the horrible sensation of her own fire wash through her. The pain was terrible. Recovering her wits, Destiny reached up with one of her claws and struck this second gryphon, easily dislodging the creature. In the meantime, Eldon had circled back, ready for more.

This was too much for Destiny. Already wounded and unable to use her fiery breath, this had suddenly become a fair fight. She had not survived this long by fighting fair. Her roar echoed off the cliffs as she streaked away to her new lair to nurse her wounds, leaving the gryphons far behind.

Dragons have long memories. Destiny would not forget this attack. When she had recovered, she would be back—back for vengeance and for blood.

***

When Gwendolyn and Polonius left the courtyard, they continued to inspect their surroundings. Save for a few storm clouds, the sky was still empty. They were safe for now. The castle and village, however, were both heavily damaged. It was obvious that Ballan á Moor could no longer be defended from Sköll's fleet when it arrived.

But Gwendolyn didn't care about that. Only her brother mattered right now. Had he survived? She closed her eyes. "Where are you?" she wondered. Then she saw an image of Aethelred in her mind. He was trapped among many stones but he was still breathing. Her eyes blinked open. How did she know that? It wasn't important right now. She had to reach him. Stumbling forward, she picked her way across the rubble.

"Where are you going?" she heard Polonius ask. She paid no attention. She could feel Aethelred's presence. He was near. Soon, she arrived at a large pile of stones and wooden beams. He was here. She struggled to tear away the stones. "Help me!" she cried.

Polonius joined her and they both dug frantically at the debris under their feet. After a few moments, they heard a muffled cry and recognized the voice immediately. "Aethelred!" Gwendolyn shouted. Drawing on strength she did not know she had, Gwendolyn furiously began casting large stones aside. Then she saw a hand. "We're here, Aethelred! We're here!" she said. "We're coming!" In a few more minutes, the girl and her tutor pulled the boy out of the rubble. He lay under a large wooden doorframe, which had saved his life when the wall collapsed.

Gwendolyn hugged him hard and did not want to let go. "Are you okay?" she asked, still clutching him.

He grinned weakly. "I would be if I were able to breathe."

She let her brother go and looked at him closely. At least he hadn't lost his sense of humor. Other than a few small scrapes and bruises, he was unhurt.

"Really, I'm fine," he whispered, stepping backwards. Then, he noticed the destruction all around them. The sight of the dead half-buried in the rubble was too much for him.

She hugged him close again. "Don't look," she said. "We're safe now."

After a moment, Aethelred let her go and wiped away his tears. "What happened?" Gwendolyn explained that she and Polonius escaped through the hatch in his room and used the tunnel near the stables to re-emerge. "Tunnels?" He wanted to know more but suddenly he looked troubled. "Where are mother and father?" Gwendolyn's mind raced. Where had she last seen them?

"They must have been in the castle—along with your uncle—when the dragon attacked," said Polonius, looking worried. "If they survived, they'll be looking for you, too."

If they survived? Gwendolyn hadn't considered that. What if her parents were dead? What would she and Aethelred do? She didn't allow herself to think of such things. Besides, there were almost certainly more people still alive buried beneath the rubble. They looked around the ruined landscape and saw that they were not alone. Dozens of villagers who had managed to survive the dragon's wrath were anxiously searching for others. At Polonius's prompting, Gwendolyn and Aethelred put aside their anxiety, and joined the search.

It was terrible work. Many of those still alive were badly hurt while others were simply too frightened to move. Working together with the villagers, Polonius and the children helped them out of the rubble and attended to their wounds. When they could find no one else, they began collecting pieces of wood to build stretchers for those unable to walk.

A short time later, Polonius cried out. "Gwendolyn! Aethelred! Look!" Gwendolyn followed her tutor's gaze. Her father and Uncle Wulfric approached them slowly on horseback. They had survived! But her heart quickly sank. Where was her mother?

"Father!" yelled Aethelred. The boy burst into tears as he ran to the king. Gwendolyn followed, holding back tears herself. She had been brave until now. When she saw her father, however, her stoicism crumbled like the castle's stone walls. Argus dismounted and hugged them closely.

His eyes were wild with a mixture of grief and joy as he stared down at them. "Are you hurt?" Sobbing into his father's chest, Aethelred was unable to speak.

"No, father," replied Gwendolyn, wiping away tears. "We're both fine."

Then she noticed her father had tears in his eyes, too. Gwendolyn had never seen him cry before. Over his shoulder, she smiled faintly at her uncle, who remained on his horse. There was dried blood on Wulfric's face but he did not look badly wounded. He winked at her before his gaze returned to the horizon. Gone was the laughter that she was accustomed to seeing in her uncle's eyes. Instead, she saw deep anger.

"And you, Polonius?" The king had seen the old man as if for the first time. "Are you wounded?"

"No, my lord," declared Polonius.

By this time, many of the villagers had gathered around them in a circle, looking frightened and confused, as they awaited the king's direction. Argus told them to make for the forest where a camp was being assembled.

"Where is mother?" cried Aethelred. "I want to see her."

"She's well," the king responded, cradling his son's face in both hands. "She's in the forest with the rest of our people, tending the wounded. She'll be much better, however, when she knows you're both safe."

"We would all be safer," added Wulfric, scanning the skies, "if we didn't remain exposed for too long."

"Agreed," declared Argus. "Come, everyone." Argus and Wulfric let two of the villagers who were limping from their injuries use their horses while they held the reins and walked along side of them.

"What will we do for protection?" asked Gwendolyn, looking back at the ruin that was once Ballan á Moor. "The Merovian fleet will be here soon. How will we defend ourselves?"

"We will make do in the forest for now," said her father, putting his hand on her shoulder. "At least the trees can give us cover."

"Besides," said Wulfric, smiling now for the first time, "the dragon will be the least of your father's worries if he doesn't take you to your mother immediately."

***

When they had reached the forest a short while later, Gwendolyn saw that a make-shift camp had been assembled, with dozens of tents erected under the thick canopy of trees. Scores of villagers and soldiers filled the tents, many of them wounded, while others hurriedly attended to them. Gwendolyn looked up at the dense network of branches above. It might provide cover, she thought, but it wouldn't stop the dragon if she decided to return.

Then Gwendolyn saw her mother. The queen was washing and bandaging the arm of an olive-skinned boy who looked about Gwendolyn's age. He must be the Merovian her uncle had spoken about, she thought.

"Gwendolyn! Aethelred!" cried the queen, racing up and embracing her children. Her eyes were red from weeping.

"They're unhurt," the king assured her. "We found them with Polonius." When Gwendolyn turned back to look at the boy her mother had been helping, he was gone.

"Oh, Polonius!" said Thelda, relieved. "Thank you!" She kissed him on the cheek, much to his embarrassment.

"It was nothing your highness," he replied, blushing. "They were both very brave."

"Brave—and lucky," declared Wulfric. "If the gryphons hadn't arrived, the dragon could have done much more damage. I saw the beast settle near your room, Polonius. I still don't understand how you survived."

Polonius looked uncomfortable. "We went . . . underground, sire."

The queen looked horrified. "Do you mean in the tunnels?" She turned to her husband. "I thought those passageways had been sealed?" The children listened intently. Their parents also knew about the tunnels?

"Most of them have been," answered Polonius.

"Most?" The queen's frown deepened. "They aren't safe, Polonius!"

"He did the right thing, based on the circumstances, Thelda," said the king. Then, turning to the old man, Argus continued. "But we mustn't press our luck underneath the castle." Gwendolyn guessed that her father meant more by those words than he cared to acknowledge openly.

"I don't think luck has anything to do with it," replied Gwendolyn, remembering the beast's strange words.

"What do you mean?" asked her mother.

"The dragon was looking for something," Gwendolyn explained. She shuddered, remembering those cruel eyes. "She demanded I help her find something." Now it was Argus's turn to look surprised. He exchanged worried glances with Thelda.

"She?" Wulfric looked puzzled. "How do you know the dragon is female?"

Gwendolyn thought about it. How did she know? "I'm . . . I'm not sure."

Her uncle continued to stare at her. "What would this dragon want with you?"

"I don't know," she responded, just as confused as her uncle. "I can only tell you what happened." Her parents and uncle marveled as Gwendolyn recounted her experience with the dragon. (Polonius noticed that she neglected to include the unusual way in which she had saved her brother's life, but he said nothing.) Then Wulfric described the battle in the sky above Ballan á Moor before the dragon disappeared over the horizon, followed by the gryphons.

"We certainly owe Eldon and Khailen our gratitude," said the king.

"Khailen?" asked Gwendolyn. "Is that the name of the other gryphon?"

"Yes," explained her father. "Gryphons are strange creatures, coming and going as they please. I hadn't seen Eldon in years before today. However, they saved our lives. We must not forget them."

The queen looked up at her husband hopefully. "Does this mean you will reconsider Eldon's counsel and make peace with the giants?"

Argus shook his head. "Impossible."

"Please, Argus," she begged. "We need their help now more than ever."

Argus looked at her and smiled sadly. "You don't understand, my love. The giants would ask me for something that I could not give. I am afraid we must look after ourselves."

Suddenly, Gwendolyn felt dizzy. She took a slight step forward to catch herself and felt two strong arms steady her. "I've got you!" said her father's voice, gently. "What were we thinking keeping you here? You and Aethelred need rest."

Her father carried her into a tent, furnished with some rugs, chairs, and cushions salvaged from the castle. He laid her down gently. The queen followed, clutching Aethelred, and put him down next to his sister. "Rest now," said the king to both of them. "We will be back to check on you later."

"Where are you going?" wondered Gwendolyn. The thought of losing her parents had made her realize how deeply she needed them.

"We must continue to look for more survivors," said her father. "I cannot rest until I know that everyone is accounted for." Then, seeing the worry on her face, he mustered a smile. "There is hope yet," he added. "We may have found a boy who can command the loyalty of a good portion of the Merovian fleet."

"What of the tunnels you spoke of earlier?" asked Aethelred. "Can't we go there?"

Argus and Thelda looked uncomfortably at one another. Finally, the king shook his head. "No, Aethelred," he said. "If we took refuge in the tunnels, the Merovians would be able to corner us much more easily. Even if I convinced our people to descend below the castle, I could not do so in good conscience for the catacombs come with their own set of dangers. Now rest."

"I will have some food brought to you," added the queen, kissing them both on the head. Argus took Thelda's hand and led her out of the tent. The children, exhausted, were soon asleep.

6

BURIED TREASURE

When Gwendolyn opened her eyes again the tent was dim. Annoyed with herself for sleeping so long, she felt for her brother who had been lying next to her. "Aethelred, wake up," she whispered. "The sun must have set." But he was gone. Only the pillows and blankets remained. He must have thought she needed the rest.

Rising, she walked to the entrance of the tent and pushed past the flaps—and was immediately sorry she had done so. She was standing in almost total darkness. At first, she thought it was merely evening. Where, however, were the stars? And where was everyone else?

Then, to her astonishment, she saw a snake seemingly made of fire slithering its way toward her. She blinked, and saw more clearly. It wasn't a snake, she realized, but a line of perhaps fifty torches approaching her in the distance. The forest had disappeared, along with her parents and the rest of the refugees who had gathered outside. Instead, the torchlight danced upon the ceiling and walls of what looked like a large cave or tunnel that surrounded her. Was she underground? As the torches came closer, she saw that they were held by large hands covered in rough, scaly skin. The next moment, she could make out the green, disfigured faces of trolls.

Despite her fear, Gwendolyn was fascinated by the variety of their features. Some of the trolls had long, wolf-like snouts. Others had flat faces and hideously misshapen jaws and lips pierced with golden rings. Still others had deep-set eyes and long, flared nostrils that resembled some of the gargoyles she had seen on Valmar's walls. Many of the creatures bore tattoos of what looked like the moon. But all of them had sharp teeth and wild, restless eyes.

Then they began to sing. At first, she thought they were just grunting. As she listened more closely, however, she could make out words, despite their harsh, guttural voices.

Trudge, trudge, past rock and mud,
Make no sound, spill no blood.
Dig, dig, through clay and stone
Underneath Childeric's throne.
Seek, seek, the sleeping seed,
feel its power, sense its greed.
Find, find the buried prize
But do not look into its eyes!
Wait, wait. He'll tame it soon
And usher in Valmar's doom!

Gwendolyn pondered the meaning of these words when she realized the trolls had spotted her. The leader snarled, and he began running toward her. She turned and ran blindly, holding her hands out before her, desperate to escape down the winding tunnel. The path diverged into two and sometimes even three separate avenues, but she continued down the central corridor. The torches of her pursuers helped illuminate her path, but she could still barely see what was ahead of her. She turned a corner and looked back but the torchlight disappeared along with the shouts from the trolls. At the same moment, she saw light up ahead and heard more voices.

Creeping up the path, Gwendolyn was more confused than ever. Where was she? What had become of the trolls? She walked forward a short distance and noticed that the light had grown brighter. Then the tunnel ended abruptly, opening into an enormous circular cavern that dropped away before her. She looked down upon a group of trolls with picks and shovels. They were busily digging and hauling away large rocks and rough earth below her. The walls of the cavern were lit by many torches and she could see that the entrance from which she overlooked the area was one of many tunnels that fed into this place. Based on the number of entrances at different levels of this large chamber, it looked as though the trolls had started digging from above, and worked their way down in corkscrew fashion.

Then she looked up and saw something odd. She expected to see an uneven, earthen ceiling that matched the cavern's roughly hewn walls. Instead, she saw large slabs of smoothly polished tiles and wood that had been unearthed and now ribbed the jagged ceiling. She wanted to study the ceiling in more detail, but her attention was drawn to the trolls at the bottom of the space when she heard their voices.

"I told you we're digging in the wrong place!" grunted a large, black troll with gold hoops in his ears. He was holding a shovel and speaking to another, smaller troll with a mohawk. "We should have found it by now." Some of the others around him stopped digging, and nodded in agreement.

"Maybe you would have found it by now if you were doing less complaining—and more digging!" spat the smaller troll, contemptuously. If he was scared of the larger troll, Gwendolyn thought, he didn't show it.

The larger troll was unimpressed. "You've been telling us that for months," he scoffed, looking at his fellow diggers, and pointing to the smaller troll. "First he said it would be at the bottom of the well, so we swam to the bottom but found nothing. Then we excavated the area under the entire courtyard. Still nothing. Now we've dug under half the area of Ballan á Moor itself. How do we know these wretched Valmarians haven't moved it?"

"Because the master says it's here," said the smaller troll, sharply. "He's never wrong." Suddenly, he changed his tone. "But perhaps you'd like to take your complaints to him yourself?" he added sarcastically. The larger troll looked nervous as the smaller one continued. "I'm sure he would love to explain himself to the likes of you."

The larger troll's eyes widened in alarm. "No, that's not necessary."

"Then keep digging!" snarled the smaller troll. The others jumped and quickly went back to their work.

Gwendolyn heard more voices behind her, back up the tunnel from which she had come. She saw more torchlight illuminating the passageway as the voices approached but there was nowhere for her to hide. The only way out was through the hole from which she had been spying on the trolls—and that was quite a drop. Then she saw them. Three large trolls rounded the corner, filling the passageway, and grinning wickedly.

"I thought I heard a rat," laughed the first troll.

"Me too," said the second. "But they're usually not this big."

The third grabbed Gwendolyn and hoisted her above his thick, gnarled shoulders. "Come," he said. "We haven't had fresh meat in weeks. Let's make some rat stew!" She screamed and struggled against the rough hands, pushing them away but there was no hope of overcoming the troll's strength.

"Gwendolyn! Wake up! Wake up!"

Gwendolyn opened her eyes and saw Aethelred's anxious face as he shook her awake. She was back in the tent. She could still see the afternoon sun gleaming through the canvas. It had only been a dream.

Her brother looked down at her, worried. "Are you alright?"

"Yes," she replied, sitting up, now very much relieved.

"You woke me up by thrashing about," he explained. "That must have been some dream."

"Not a dream," she said. "A nightmare." Gwendolyn leaned forward and tilted her head until it was touching Aethelred's shoulder. She let out a deep sigh. So much had happened since this morning—the appearance of the gryphon, Uncle Wulfric's return and, of course, the dragon. Perhaps that was a dream, too?

"Do you think the dragon will return, Gwen?" asked Aethelred, as if guessing her thoughts.

"Yes," she answered quietly. That might not be what he wanted to hear, but she refused to lie to him. "I'm almost sure of it. She needs me somehow."

"Needs you for what?" he asked.

"To find her seed," came a deep voice from behind them.

Gwendolyn and Aethelred both gasped as a tall, black-cloaked figure entered the tent and let the flap fall behind him. He was holding a large basket. His hood shrouded his face in darkness and he had to remain hunched over because he was too tall to stand upright. He bent down and placed the basket at their feet. As he did so, they saw that he also wore a battle axe strapped across his back. The children scrambled away, frightened.

"Don't be afraid," said the stranger.

Gwendolyn jumped to her feet. "Who are you?"

He pushed back his hood, revealing his face. "Am I so hard to recognize now that I am prepared for battle?" he asked, with the merest hint of a smile.

"Polonius!" shouted the children, greatly relieved.

He grinned but Gwendolyn could see the fatigue in his face. "You will find food in the basket," he said, sitting down next to them. "Eat quickly. We haven't much time." Aethelred dumped out the contents of the basket. It included dried sausage, apples, hard biscuits, and two waterskins. When they smelled the food, the children realized they hadn't eaten for hours and ate heartily.

"What did you mean?" asked Gwendolyn, her mouth full of apple slices. "About the dragon needing my help to find her seed?"

Polonius pulled out his pipe and began filling it with tobacco. "I believe it is the same seed your great-grandfather found long ago," he explained. "She is looking for it—and for you."

"Childeric found a dragon's seed?" she asked, intrigued. "Where is it now?"

"No one knows," responded Polonius. "It has been sought by many including your ancestors and the

Western Giants, but it has never been found." She thought he wanted to say more but he remained silent.

"I don't understand," she objected. "Why have you never told us this before?"

"I'm telling you now," snapped the old man, impatiently. "Mind you, I could be wrong. However, based on what I saw you do this morning—how you saved your brother's life—I think you share the dragon seed's magic. The great serpent is drawn to you, Gwendolyn."

Aethelred stopped eating and looked at his sister nervously. "Gwen, you know . . . magic?"

"No!" she insisted. "I can hardly remember dates and names. How could I memorize spells?"

"Your sister is not a magician," explained Polonius, looking past Aethelred as if trying to remember things that had fled his memory years ago. "However, she was born with magical power."

"Me?" Gwendolyn was incredulous. "How?"

"Young dragons have very powerful magic," explained Polonius, puffing on his pipe. "Their magic is even more potent when they have yet to hatch. Your great-grandfather must have absorbed some of its power when he touched the egg. In each generation since, the first-born of Childeric's descendants has inherited this power in some measure."

"The dragon senses this power in me?" asked Gwendolyn, horrified, as she remembered the untamed feeling that seemed to flow through her when the dragon attacked.

Her tutor studied her for a moment. "I'm afraid so."

Gwendolyn shook her head. "I never asked for this!"

"There are many things we get that we never ask for," said Polonius, without pity. "And some things we ask for we never get." Gwendolyn simply glared at her tutor. She hated it when he spoke like this.

"Wait a minute," said Aethelred, confused. "Our father was first-born. He never mentioned this power."

"No," replied Polonius, sadly. "Your father wouldn't have mentioned it because he never truly believed." Seeing the confused looks on the children's faces, he continued. "When the king was about your age, Gwendolyn, he began to sense this power lived in him. As his tutor, I tried to help him master the dragon magic but he grew afraid—afraid of being different. So he ignored it and pretended it never existed. Now the magic lies dormant in him. I doubt he could awaken it again even if he tried."

Gwendolyn put her head in her hands Things were changing so fast. How could she hope to understand it all? "Why are we learning this now?" she demanded, angry that this knowledge had been kept from her.

"I had been waiting for you to grow older before trying to explain these matters," explained the old man. "However, I'm afraid we've run out of time. Like it or not, you are heir to a portion of Destiny's power."

"I don't believe in destiny," grumbled Gwendolyn, dismissively. "We make our own way in this world."

"You're not listening," replied Polonius, raising his voice. "Destiny is the dragon's *name*."

Gwendolyn looked up at her tutor and her eyes widened. "The dragon's *name*?" she said. "How do you know that?"

"She is infamous among the giants," he responded. "You see, she has lived for more than a thousand years and in that time, she has killed many things, including them."

"You never mentioned her in my history lessons," objected Aethelred. "I only know of a dragon named Cynder."

"That was her mate, I believe," said Polonius. "The giants killed him when Childeric was a young man. However, I suspect she has other mates—and other lairs—beyond our shores."

"All the same," replied Aethelred, "I would have liked to learn more about dragons—especially now."

Gwendolyn agreed. She regretted that she had not read more history books like her brother. But even he had no knowledge of Destiny's existence. They both had to rely upon Polonius to tell them the truth. Why had the old man kept all of this a secret until now? She stared at him, upset. "What else haven't you told us, Polonius?"

"I'm sorry, my dear," he mumbled. "The king forbade me to speak of it."

She folder her arms. "Why?"

"He insisted the story of Destiny's lost seed was a fable," he explained. "You must understand—until today, a dragon had not been seen in almost a hundred years. Argus refused to allow me to mention her story—especially when it came to his own children. He did not want your head filled with foolish stories."

Aethelred grinned slightly. "I'll bet he doesn't believe it's foolish now."

"I still don't understand," declared Gwendolyn. "Why hasn't the seed hatched?"

Polonius shifted uncomfortably. "Dragon seeds can lay dormant for centuries," he said. "They only hatch when exposed to dragon fire."

"That sounds strange," stated Aethelred. "Wouldn't fire destroy them?"

"Many things are strange about dragons," replied the old man, "for they are magical creatures." Polonius sighed when he saw the children's faces still clouded in confusion. "This process is not unique to dragons. Think of pine cones. They fall to the forest floor and do not germinate until a forest fire consumes the shell."

"I see," nodded Gwendolyn. "Only when the shell is destroyed can the seed hatch."

"Exactly," said Polonius. "All living things—including children and dragons—must become what they were meant to be—or return to dust." He extinguished his pipe. "Now, that's enough questions for one evening, if you please. We have already tarried here too long. We are still very much in danger."

Aethelred settled back on his pillow. "What do you mean?" he asked, nibbling on a biscuit. "The gryphons drove Destiny away."

Polonius looked at him impatiently. "Do you really think she won't come back? Gryphons are fierce adversaries. The dragon, however, won't underestimate them again—assuming we are lucky enough to have their help a second time."

"He's right," replied Gwendolyn, pushing her hair back behind her ears, and now looking very grown up. "If Destiny is drawn to the magic in me, the forest is no defense. Every moment I remain here, I put our people in danger." She faced Polonius. "What do you propose we do?"

"Go underground," he said. "Only then will we be safe from the dragon."

"Underground?" Aethelred looked frightened. "Father said the tunnels underneath the castle are dangerous."

"They can be," admitted Polonius. "However, there are other tunnels which are safer."

Gwendolyn remembered how Polonius had easily led her through the maze of tunnels just a few short hours ago underneath Ballan á Moor. "What's so dangerous about the passageway that you and I were in?"

Polonius rose and stared down at the children. "Many of the tunnels underneath the castle can go very deep," he said, "though most of the entrances to them have been sealed. One could easily get lost in the catacombs without a guide for they were built to confuse those not meant to use them."

"Is that why father had them closed?" asked Gwendolyn.

The old man nodded his head. "When your father became king, he ordered his engineers and stone masons to collapse parts of the tunnel, making it impassable. In that way, he blocked most entrances."

"Not all of them, it would seem," she returned, smiling slightly at the old man and remembering the trap door underneath his great desk when Destiny had attacked. He shrugged his shoulder and sheepishly returned her smile.

Aethelred was still nervous at the thought of going underground. "Mother and father would want us to stay here," he objected.

"Then we'd better not ask," declared Gwendolyn. "I refuse to put our people in danger by staying here. Aeth, you don't have to —"

"You're not getting rid of me that easily," he snapped, rising and trying to sound braver than he felt. "Besides, how could I live with myself if I couldn't follow a girl into the darkness?"

"Come," said Polonius. "I know of another way to reach the tunnels without risking the open sky." Then, reaching into his cloak, he produced two small leather bags and gave one to each child. Gwendolyn and Aethelred gathered apples, biscuits, dried sausage, and two full waterskins into the sacks, and flung them over their shoulders. "There is an entrance not very far from here," added the old man. "Follow me." He led the way out of the back of the tent and into the forest as the children followed closely behind.

Gwendolyn took one long look back at the camp. It was now late afternoon. People sat huddled together closely in the forest, talking in low tones, while others still tended to the wounded. (They did not dare light campfires for fear of attracting the dragon.) Gwendolyn knew her parents would never consent to her journey, but she refused to risk another one of Destiny's attacks because of the burden she now carried within her. She turned and followed Polonius and Aethelred past the clearing and into the woods.

As soon as they were out of sight, a figure detached itself from the shadows and quietly followed them.

7

UP AND UNDER

As the sun sank toward the horizon, Polonius and the children made their way south, deeper into the woods along a narrow path. Gwendolyn was struck by how quiet things had become now that they were well beyond the camp. Usually, one could hear a chorus of birds in the trees or see squirrels dashing about in the branches above. Now, however, an eerie silence pervaded the forest. All she seemed to hear were Polonius's heavy footsteps, but even those were dampened by the pine needles covering the ground. Perhaps a storm was coming, she thought. Or, more likely, the dragon's scent had caused all of the forest's creatures to scatter. Whatever the reason, she felt alone and it made her want to fill the silence with words.

"Polonius?" she said, hurrying to keep pace with the large man.

"Yes?"

"What did you mean earlier when you said that my ancestors and the giants had both looked for Destiny's seed? Where did they look and what did they hope to find?"

Polonius shifted the straps that held his battle axe across his back. "Don't you remember your history lessons?" he asked. "When the giants helped Childeric and his men build the castle's foundations, they also sought a treasure."

"I remember," she replied. "You called it a peculiar treasure but you didn't say what it was. It's the seed, isn't it?"

Polonius sighed and nodded his head. "I believe so."

"Why did they fight over it?" asked Aethelred. "What did the giants hope to gain?"

"What most creatures wish to gain," declared the old man. "Power."

Aethelred glanced at his sister. "What sort of power?"

"According to legend, those with the seed's power can wield the same magic as the dragons," explained Polonius. "But only after spending years learning how to control it."

Aethelred stopped. "You mean Gwendolyn can breathe fire?"

Despite himself, Polonius laughed grimly. "No," he said, stopping and facing the boy. "After much practice, however, Childeric and Edubard could transfix others with a stare. Or control weak-willed people with a mere suggestion. Then there was the death song."

Gwendolyn frowned. "The death song?"

"History really isn't your best subject, is it?" scolded her tutor. Gwendolyn looked embarrassed and was about to defend herself but Aethelred spoke first. "It involves our grandfather, Edubard. The giants called him something strange. What was it?" His eyes brightened. "Oh yes! Edubard the Enchanter."

Polonius nodded and continued walking, followed by the children. "That was one of the names men called him," he said. "To enchant can mean to put one under a spell—or to break it. However, it's always done through song—which is what enchantment means. Edubard wielded the death song ruthlessly, I'm afraid."

Gwendolyn smiled admiringly. "He must have been dreadful in battle."

"He was," recalled Polonius. "Edubard used this magic to kill many trolls when giants and men were allies. It was Edubard who drove the trolls back to the Solitary Marshes, and made the forest safe again—at least for a time." Polonius paused for a moment, as if remembering something that troubled him. "But using that power also changed him—made him harder. When he turned on the giants, and used the death-song against them, he had become someone wholly different from the man he once was."

Gwendolyn remembered how she had saved her brother from being crushed by the falling stones when Destiny had burst into Polonius's study that morning. She looked up and saw Polonius staring at her beneath his large, white eyebrows. She looked away uncomfortably though she didn't quite understand why.

"Then we must find the seed and destroy it somehow," said Aethelred, firmly. "One dragon prowling the skies is enough—we don't need another."

As her brother spoke those words, Gwendolyn felt sick. Why? She had no reason to feel protective of a beast she had never met. Especially an unborn dragon. Yet for all of the danger it could pose, she felt sure that no harm should come to the creature. She also became momentarily angry when Aethelred suggested they destroy the seed. Had she not used its magic to save his life? Would he be so quick to kill something that possessed a power that could be used against his enemies?

"Is there no other way?" she asked, irritably. "Assuming we could even find the seed?"

A thought began to grow in her mind, though she was afraid to speak it. As Childeric's heir, why should she not harness more of the seed's power for herself? According to Polonius, Childeric only possessed the seed for a short time, and inherited some of the dragon's power. What would happen if Gwendolyn were to possess it for good? Might she grow to be greater than Childeric or even Edubard the Enchanter? What would stop her from defeating Sköll's army and perhaps even Destiny herself?

She day-dreamed again of her father challenging Sköll to single combat, only now the person in the armor was not her father—but herself. Her white horse snorted impatiently as she sat upon his back, arrayed in golden armor, holding her father's sword. Then, she raised her visor to show the Merovian king and all of his soldiers her face before she destroyed them with a single word. How wonderful that would be! To drive all of Valmar's enemies before her! To free her people! To be worshipped by all!

Suddenly, she grew troubled. When she had cried out in grief and fear during Destiny's attack—when she had saved her brother's life—she had also felt a consciousness for the first time that was not her own, responding to her call. The unborn dragon's thoughts appeared in her mind, probing her, trying to discover who and what she was. For better or for worse, she shared its power now—the same power that her great-grandfather had taken from it so long ago. Wasn't it wrong to use it in such a way?

Polonius abruptly halted in a clearing of pine trees and held up his hand. The children stopped, too, and became silent. Did a shadow move behind the trees far off the path?

"What is it?" whispered Aethelred.

"I believe we're being observed," said Polonius, looking slowly around them.

Gwendolyn followed his gaze but saw nothing. "By whom?"

The old man never glanced away from the trees. "Centaurs, if I'm not mistaken."

Gwendolyn took a step closer to the old man. She had read enough to know that centaurs were reclusive creatures that seldom left the woods. They were not wicked like trolls and ogres, but neither did they love men or involve themselves in men's affairs, preferring instead to act as caretakers of the forest and the creatures who lived in it.

Once, long ago, before even Childeric's time, centaurs had befriended men, teaching them how to use mathematics and astronomy to explore the seas. The creatures became disappointed, however, when they learned that men used this knowledge to discover and eventually conquer distant lands. Now, the creatures preferred to avoid men altogether. They could still be dangerous, however, to those who dared harm the forest.

Polonius resumed his pace, followed closely by the children. "Be careful to stay on the path—and don't purposely injure any bird or beast you may see."

They continued to walk closely together, crossing small streams and climbing tall hills, while always travelling southwest, parallel to the Skelding mountains. The weak shafts of light that had once dimly illuminated the forest's leafy floor were gone now. It became increasingly difficult to see in the growing darkness as the sun sank behind the mountains. The children seldom spoke anymore for fear of attracting attention.

Gwendolyn noticed that they were no longer walking parallel to the foothills. Instead, they were going directly into them. They had been traveling for what seemed like hours but the old man continued to lead them purposefully onward. They were now at the southern edge of the woods. The mountains rose ominously in the distance. Finally, Polonius slowed and stopped abruptly. "We're here," he declared. The children looked around. All they could see were more trees. Where was the tunnel's entrance?

"Look up," he said, as if reading their minds. Polonius patted a mammoth oak tree that stood directly in front of them. Reaching up and grabbing the lowest branch, he swung himself up easily. Despite her confusion, Gwendolyn marveled at how quickly her old tutor could move. Then she remembered again how easily he had pushed the large desk across the room in the castle when Destiny had attacked. He might look old, she thought, but he was stronger and faster than one might expect. What other secrets did he keep?

Polonius lowered one of his massive hands. "Who's next?"

"I don't understand," objected Aethelred. "I thought we were going underground."

The old man smiled mysteriously. "Sometimes the quickest way up is the fastest way down."

Before the children could climb the tree, however, the forest was filled with the sound of galloping hooves. Polonius jumped down from the tree and stood in front of Gwendolyn and Aethelred, holding his battle axe in both hands. The next moment, a large male centaur thundered into view.

The children caught their breath at the sight of the creature. He had long, brown hair that flowed loosely from his head down to his bare chest and lower back. The creature held a longbow in his muscular arms, with an arrow notched at the ready, though he kept the shaft pointed downward.

What struck the children most was the centaur's strange, wild face. Usually, when one speaks of a "wild animal" one thinks of a beast that has limited intelligence and which acts unpredictably, driven by instinct. Centaurs were anything but "wild" in this sense. Unlike men, they were ancient creatures who did not view their surroundings as something to be subjugated and mastered. Rather, they sought to live in harmony with other creatures, taking only what nature afforded. They often lived for more than a century and possessed great intelligence. From the smallest flower to the greatest nebula, nothing escaped their study. And this knowledge of the world—its fierceness as well as its beauty—was reflected in their faces.

"Who are you and what is your business here so deep in the woods?" demanded the centaur sternly, looking from Polonius to the children.

The old man cleared his throat. "My name is Polonius, and this is Princess Gwendolyn and Prince Aethelred of Valmar." He lowered his weapon. "We do not mean to trespass." The accuracy of centaur archers was legendary.

Polonius knew that they would be far safer if they did not threaten the creature.

"Perhaps not," replied the centaur. "But you have not answered both of my questions."

"We seek a way underground," explained Polonius.

Gwendolyn heard another voice to her left. "As we suspected!" Suddenly, a female centaur emerged from the woods, slightly smaller than the first though no less fierce. She had long, blond hair that flowed untamed down her back. She held a two-handed sword and looked suspiciously at the group. Gwendolyn would have admired her beauty longer if she had not been too intimidated to meet the centaur's fierce gaze.

"Are you in league with trolls?" asked the female centaur, accusingly. "Why else would you choose to travel in the twilight hours?"

"We seek the Low Road," said Polonius. "Surely you remember that it was not built by evil hands." Gwendolyn and Aethelred looked at each other. The Low Road? What did their tutor mean by that? They knew, however, not to interrupt him with questions now.

"He is right," admitted the male centaur. "We are not charged with acting as gatekeepers to that ancient highway."

"Still," replied the female centaur. "Aren't there other ways to access the Low Road without disturbing the forest's peace?"

"Indeed, there are other ways," confessed Polonius. "However, we dare not risk returning to Ballan á Moor for fear of the dragon." The old man then recounted Destiny's attack earlier that morning that had left the castle in ruins. "We must find shelter underground before she returns."

"The heavens confirm your story," declared the male centaur. "We have puzzled over the recent return of a red comet that has not been seen for a century. It must signify the red worm of which you speak." He removed the arrow from the bowstring, slung the bow across his back, and bowed. "My name is Jagomo," he stated. "This is Briara." Polonius and the children bowed in return.

"I wish we could bring you better tidings," said Polonius. "The Merovian fleet approaches Valmar and will be here in two days. I am afraid that soon even the forest will not be safe."

"That is evil news," replied Jagomo. "Unfortunately, it is not the first time violence threatens to spill over into the forest on account of men." He glanced at Briara.

"Our past dealings with your kind have taught us to be suspicious," she admitted. She held Polonius's gaze for several seconds as if guessing a secret before smiling shrewdly. "Men—and other creatures. But that is your business. You are welcome to this entrance to the Low Road if it will keep you safe."

"Thank you," said Polonius. Then he remembered the traditional words when taking leave from a centaur. "May the wind be always at your back."

The centaurs smiled in spite of their stern demeanor, impressed by his knowledge of their ways. "May the sun shine warm upon your face, and the road rise to meet you," they said.

Briana approached the children. "These are dangerous times. Have you no weapons?"

Gwendolyn and Aethelred shook their heads.

The centaur produced two small blades from the gold bracers she wore on her wrists, and handed one to each child. "You may use these." Gwendolyn's weapon had a handle made of mother of pearl while Aethelred's was inlaid with obsidian. Used as daggers by the centaurs, the blades were large enough to serve as shorts swords for the children.

"Thank you," they said, admiring the well-crafted weapons.

Briana smiled. "Use them well."

Both of the creatures turned and galloped away.

The old man sighed, thankful that the encounter had gone well.

"Polonius —" began Gwendolyn.

He rolled his eyes. "Let me guess. You want to know more about the Low Road?"

She nodded.

"It is the name of the tunnel beneath us," he explained, "and beyond the dragon's reach. However, it is more than a tunnel. You will have to see it for yourself." Then, leaping up into the tree again, he stretched out his hand. "Come along."

"You first, Aeth," said Gwendolyn. She helped her brother reach the old man's hand, and Polonius easily pulled him up into the lower branches. Gwendolyn scrambled up without any help. She was, after all, an expert tree climber—and several inches taller than her brother.

Aethelred remained in a crouching position as he tried to find a better grip on the oak's huge trunk. Gwendolyn, however, was standing on a small branch, holding her hands out with perfect balance. "Now what?" she asked.

The old man grinned. "Look up."

Both children looked up and saw a round hole in the tree about six feet above them. Though previously obscured by the lower branches, it was clearly big enough for a large man to squeeze through. Where did it go? Something else also wondered where this strange opening led. Two black eyes watched them behind a tree a short distance away.

Aethelred studied the hole. "You want us to go in there?"

Polonius nodded. Gwendolyn was intrigued. "I'll go first, Aeth," she said. "Then you can come, and Polonius will follow after." The fact that he wouldn't be first or last seemed to make Aethelred feel better, so he agreed.

"It will be dark," explained Polonius. "Just go all the way down and wait for me. Do not venture far once you reach the bottom."

"As you say," replied Gwendolyn. "Follow me, Aeth."

She climbed into the large, dark hole, feeling her way downward. It was pitch black just as Polonius had said. It was also stuffy but Gwendolyn didn't have trouble breathing. Then she felt rungs. A ladder must have been built into the hollowed out tree! There was plenty of room to turn around and descend. "How marvelous!" she thought. "I wonder who built this?"

She climbed down slowly. After about twenty rungs, however, she couldn't feel anything else. Her feet simply dangled in air. "The drop could be a few feet—or a hundred," she thought with growing anxiety. Then she had an idea. Still holding on to a rung with one hand, she reached down, removed one of her shoes, and let it drop. Almost immediately she heard the shoe hit bottom. "Doesn't sound very far," she said to herself. She lowered herself down to the bottom rung and let go.

Gwendolyn dropped about three feet and landed on what felt like tightly packed dirt. She still couldn't see anything, but there was definitely a draft coming from somewhere in front of her. The place smelled musty and stale. It also felt cold and damp, and she thought she could hear the rushing of water nearby. "I wish I had a torch," she thought to herself, as she groped in the darkness for her shoe. She finally found it and slipped it back on. Then she heard Aethelred's nervous voice from above.

"Gwen? You there?"

"Yes, I'm down here."

"I can't see!"

"It's okay, just go down the ladder."

"What ladder?"

"Feel with your hands," she replied. "It doesn't go all the way down. I'm afraid you'll have to let go when you come to the bottom. But don't worry. It's only a short drop."

After some coaxing and encouraging, Aethelred was soon down in the tunnel beside his sister. Polonius quickly followed. "Everyone here?"

"Yes," said Gwendolyn. It felt strange not being able to see Polonius and her brother. "How are we supposed to see anything?"

"Just a moment," mumbled Polonius, digging through his pack. "Now where did I put my flint and torch?"

Gwendolyn felt Aethelred take her hand. She could feel him shaking in the darkness. She didn't need to see him to know that he was frightened, and she gave his hand a little squeeze to let him know she understood. Perhaps if she continued to ask Polonius questions, the sound of her voice would comfort her brother.

"What is this place, exactly?" she asked.

"The Low Road is an underground highway—or low-way, as it were," declared the old man. "In fact, it is a series of tunnels. It stretches northeast to Ballan á Moor and southwest to the mountains." Gwendolyn wondered how he knew the difference between east and west underground.

"You mean this road is miles and miles long?" she responded, amazed.

"Correct," said Polonius. "The Low Road and its network of passageways probably span more than one hundred miles. Only the giants would know the exact distance."

"The giants?" Aethelred's voice trembled slightly. "They know about this place?"

"It was the giants who built them—as trade routes when they traded freely with men," said Polonius. "It is safer than walking through the deeper parts of the forest, especially after nightfall. Ah, here we are."

A few sparks appeared in the darkness. The next moment, the old man's face flickered into view as he held a torch in his hand. It was the area surrounding them, however, which took their breath away. They were on a small ledge at the top of a tiled stairway that led down to the main tunnel about twenty feet below from where they stood. The passage was enormous, stretching away into the darkness in both directions. Like the stairway, it was tiled both above and below with a type of stone, smooth and red, that Gwendolyn didn't recognize. In some places on the ceiling, gnarled tree roots had forced their way through the tiles, and hung down like vines.

The most startling discovery, however, was the river that flowed parallel to the path a few yards away. Attached to the embankment near where they stood was a pier that jutted out into the water. Unfortunately, there were no signs of any boats. Now she understood why

Polonius had told her not to move once she reached the tunnel. The water looked swift.

"A river?" cried Gwendolyn. "Underground?"

"Why not?" replied Polonius. "Do you think rivers only travel above ground? I was hoping a boat would be here but we'll manage on foot. Come along."

Still holding hands, Gwendolyn and Aethelred followed the old man down the stairs to the Low Road. "Where does the river lead?" she asked.

Polonius looked back at them. "It stretches from north to south, flowing from the Skeldings toward Ballan á Moor. In fact, the river even passes underneath the castle to the sea." As he held up the torch in front of him, its light cast shadows on the walls, making the roots above look like snakes. She examined her brother. Aethelred had become pale and silent. If the place was unsettling to her, what must he be feeling? She stopped when they had reached the bottom of the stairs.

"Polonius," she said, firmly. "Aethelred and I have followed you patiently out of camp, through the forest, and into this tunnel. We are now below ground and safe—I hope—from that horrid dragon for the moment. Now I must ask you a question, and I demand an answer."

She had learned so many strange things since awakening that we must forgive her if she sounded a bit rude. Polonius straightened his glasses and looked at her, a bit startled. "What is it princess?"

"How did you know about this tunnel?" she asked. "How did you know about the tunnels underneath Ballan á Moor? Why have you never told us before?"

The old man looked a bit sheepish. "Oh dear, I suppose you deserve an answer." He removed his glasses and began polishing them on his cloak. "I was shown the Low Road when I was still very young."

"Shown?" wondered Aethelred. "Who showed it to you?"

"The giants," replied Polonius.

The children gasped. "What?" cried Gwendolyn. "You've had dealings with giants?"

Polonius stopped what he was doing and looked up. He let out a deep, slow breath. "Well, now we come to it," he said, smiling meekly. "You see, I am a quarter-giant. One of the last of my kind."

8

CHILDERIC'S RIDDLE

Polonius gazed down at the children in silence as the torch flickered in his hand. There was nowhere for them to run and no one to whom they could call for help. For better or worse, he held the only light in the darkness.

Aethelred's fingers tightened on the hilt of his sword while he studied the large man that stood before them. "Don't make jokes," he warned. "I'm frightened enough."

Gwendolyn, however, could see that Polonius wasn't joking. She looked at him as if for the first time. Why had she never seen it before? True, he was very tall, but there were many tall men among the Valmarians. That didn't necessarily make him a quarter-giant though, but when she thought about it, he was easily the tallest person she had ever met. Then she also noticed his large hands and feet. They were big—too big for a man. What really convinced her, however, were his teeth. She remembered that giants had sharp teeth. Not jagged and hideous like trolls but sharp enough to be clearly different from human teeth. While his teeth were not nearly as sharp as someone with full giant blood, they were oddly pointed. Gwendolyn realized this was why he seldom smiled.

Polonius could see the alarm in the children's eyes. "Do not be afraid," he exclaimed, hastily. "I also have human blood in my veins. I think you'll find that we are really quite peaceful."

"How is that possible?" Gwendolyn asked, dumbfounded by the sudden revelation.

"What I taught you about the ancient friendship between giants and men holds true," he explained. "I was born shortly before the Giant Wars, when giants and men were still allies. I am living proof that we need not be enemies."

Aethelred stepped behind his sister and drew his sword clumsily. Gwendolyn knew she had to act quickly before he panicked and did something rash. First, however, she had to know if they were in danger.

"What is your true purpose for taking us down here, Polonius?" she demanded, narrowing her eyes.

Polonius looked hurt. "Your safety—and the safety of Valmar—has always been my primary concern," he said indignantly. "I have served your family for three generations, and I assure you that you're much safer here than in the camp. A few trees will not stop Destiny." Then he sighed, and sat down wearily on one of the earthen steps. "I confess, however, that I still have not told you all."

She put her hands on her hips as Aethelred peeked out from behind her. "This is your chance."

The old man handed her the torch and rubbed his face. "Now that we're underground, Destiny can no longer threaten us," he explained. "However, we can also use the Low Road to return to Ballan á Moor—or at least to the tunnels directly underneath the castle."

"The catacombs," recalled Gwendolyn. "Why would we want to go there?"

"That is where I believe the seed lies."

"The seed that was lost?" Aethelred gulped. "The seed—of Destiny?"

"Correct," replied Polonius. "Though some believe it hasn't been lost so much as it has been cunningly hidden."

Aethelred frowned. Despite his fear, he was very curious. "From whom?"

"From anyone who seeks to abuse its power," said Polonius. "As I told you, the giants claimed that Childeric had promised them the seed in return for helping him build Ballan á Moor and defeating the trolls. He very well may have. I suspect that as he grew older, however, Childeric feared the seed's power. Feared it— and had it jealously guarded. After all, the catacombs were your great-grandfather's idea."

Gwendolyn's eyes grew round. "That's why the catacombs are so confusing," she said, excitedly. "They are meant to keep people from finding the seed of Destiny."

Polonius nodded. "Edubard and others searched under Ballan á Moor for years but without success. In fact, many brave knights ventured into that labyrinth never to be seen again. Argus had the tunnels closed when he became king to discourage the practice."

Gwendolyn thought of her father with a glimmer of admiration. "He was protecting us—all of us."

"I'm afraid the catacombs are only the beginning," stated Polonius. "Power has a way of attracting evil things—especially in the dark places of the world. We may not be alone under the foundations of the castle. I tell this to you not to frighten you, but to let you decide for yourselves whether you want to continue—or remain here."

Aethelred looked at his sister. "This just gets better and better," he said, rolling his eyes. Gwendolyn smiled. Her brother's sarcasm showed that he had overcome his initial fear of Polonius's true identity. She had to admit that it would have been impossible for their tutor to reveal that he was a quarter-giant to the people of Valmar. Many of the villagers would have run screaming at the very thought of a giant living in their midst.

Gwendolyn handed the torch back to Polonius and put her hand on the hilt of her sword. "Well, we're certainly not going to sit here like rabbits in a hole while Destiny terrorizes our people—and Sköll's navy prepares to attack a second time," she declared firmly.

Aethelred looked at his sister and smirked. "You certainly have a talent for attracting evil. It would be a shame to waste it."

She smiled. Yes, she thought. Quite a talent. What other talents might she possess if she could find the seed? Gwendolyn remembered that Eldon had urged her to make peace with the giants before Sköll attacked. But perhaps she didn't need the giants help after all? She could simply borrow more of the seed's power until the threat was destroyed. She wouldn't harm it by doing so, would she?

Gwendolyn looked at Polonius. "Our only chance now is to find the seed and use it before someone else does."

Aethelred's smirk vanished. "What about destroying it?"

"I'm not sure we could," replied the old man. "Dragon shells are stronger than any other known material." Then, turning to Gwendolyn, he continued. "A dragon seed contains a tremendous amount of power, Gwendolyn. Do you really think you could wield it wisely if you possessed its full measure?"

"What other choice do we have?" she asked. "You admitted yourself that I don't have time to learn how to control the power I inherited. If I can lay my hands on the seed, perhaps it will be different. It's our only chance!"

Aethelred and Polonius looked at each other doubtfully. They had no answer, and time was running out. Polonius stood up. "I think I can get us into the catacombs from here," he said. "After that, however, I am afraid there is only Childeric's Riddle to guide us as we search for Destiny's seed."

Aethelred looked at the old man, puzzled. "You mean Childeric's Curse?"

"It is also known by that name," acknowledged Polonius, impressed that Aethelred would remember. "These days, however, men consider it only a child's nursery rhyme, nothing more."

Gwendolyn was lost. "What are you two talking about?"

"Don't you remember the rhyme Polonius taught us when we were little, Gwen?" said her brother. "The one about the sightless eyes, the abyss—and there was one more thing. What was it Polonius?"

"The thing unseen," said the old man, gloomily.

"That's right," replied Aethelred, brightening. "I like that rhyme."

Gwendolyn shook her head. "You'll have to remind me."

Aethelred looked at his tutor and smiled. "Allow me." It wasn't often that he could best his sister but he had an excellent memory, and now proved the better student. "Let me see," he mumbled, clasping his hands behind his back as if reciting a poem. "Childeric's Riddle:

If you wish to seek my prize,
disturb its rest and cause its rise
Think you twice, for deep it lies
under a ring of sightless eyes."

"Yes, I think I remember this now," said Gwendolyn. "Polonius used to sing it to me when I was very young."

"Shhh!" replied Aethelred, impatiently. "I'm not finished yet."

In an abyss of ghostly green
it rests though restless as it dreams,
Guarded by a power unseen
you must defeat to be redeemed.

But what you seek and what you find
May be different when combined.
For it will know your true design
And see your soul, though it be blind.

Gwendolyn sighed. "That makes as much sense to me now as when I first heard it."

"Those are the words that Childeric wrote shortly before he died," explained Polonius. "Though he kept the seed hidden, even he couldn't resist teasing later generations with such clues."

"What are we waiting for?" asked Aethelred. "Which way back to the castle? Or rather, under the castle?"

Polonius pointed down the tunnel in the direction behind them. "That way."

After they all had a bit of water and a couple of biscuits, they continued down the tunnel together. The way was broad and deep, allowing them to walk side by side. As they traveled, the road curved sharply downward but mostly it remained comfortably level. That was just as well for the children, who had to walk quickly to keep up with the long strides of the quarter-giant who held the torch up as he led them forward. Occasionally, they also saw other, narrower tunnels leading off to the left and right. Polonius, however, never wavered, always following the main road ahead of them.

The tunnel, it should be said, was not a dreary, dirt-packed run that you might expect snakes or rabbits to occupy. No, the Low Road was a grand tunnel made by giants—which is to say it was built to last. The passage was supported by large oak beams at regular intervals, and was wide enough for two giants to walk shoulder to shoulder. It was also covered with painted tiles depicting scenes of giants, men, trolls, and ancient battles. Polonius and the children even passed stone shelters from time to time built into the walls that looked like they had once stored food and drink to help travelers on their journey. The shelters, however, were empty, having been abandoned long ago. It was clear that the Low Road had fallen out of use, as revealed by the deep cracks in the tiles that marred the mosaics, as well as the amount of dust and debris that filled the place.

They marched along in silence just as they had in the forest. However, in contrast to the eerie stillness of the woods, the pleasant sound of rushing water kept them company as it ran parallel to the path. Nevertheless, Aethelred was disappointed that they had yet to see a boat moored to the tunnel wall.

At one point, Gwendolyn thought she recognized a scene illustrated on the faded tiles overhead. A man and a giant sat on opposite sides of a large banquet table, flanked by many others of their kind. The giant had bright green eyes and wore a gold crown. He was smiling and holding a glass of wine up to the man on the other end of the table, who also wore a crown. Everyone looked merry. Gwendolyn looked closer at the man and realized it was her great-grandfather, Childeric, seated in the Great Hall of Ballan á Moor.

They came to another scene that depicted a fierce battle in the mountains. Hundreds of men and giants clad in armor could be seen racing up a hill towards a banner emblazoned with a red skull. Underneath the banner stood many trolls armed with pikes and maces as they waited for the inevitable clash.

"Polonius," asked Gwendolyn, pointing out the mosaics. "What do these mean?"

"They memorialize events from long ago," he replied. "We must be close to home now."

As they trudged along, the scene on the walls changed again. This time they could make out a series of images. The first showed a cave filled with giants busily crafting massive shields, swords, and shining suits of giant armor that glowed in the embers of a cavernous forge. A second image revealed a lake of flame that the giants used to feed the forge. In a third scene, however,

Gwendolyn noticed that some of the giants were making smaller shields and weapons that would be much too small to use themselves.

"What are they doing making such small suits of armor?" she wondered. "They look like toys."

Polonius smiled. "Not to the brave Valmarian knights for whom they were forged," he explained. "This mosaic is to commemorate the alliance between men and giants when the troll armies attacked long ago." He looked down at the children. "Our races have not always been at odds."

Aethelred motioned to the flaming lake. "What's that in the background?" he asked. "It looks orange."

Polonius rubbed his eyes before examining the image. "I believe the giants called it Ozzo's Furnace."

"Ozzo's Furnace?" The boy looked puzzled. "What's that?"

"A cavern deep in the mountains to the west. Perhaps more importantly, it is a volcano that holds within its belly a lake of fire."

The boy looked back at the mosaic in wonder. "That doesn't sound pleasant."

"It isn't," he admitted. "Long ago, the giants used it as a forge to make tools and weapons. The greatest king and blacksmith among them, Ozzo, created suits of armor that some say could withstand dragon's fire. However, such treasures have been lost. The forge has been abandoned for many years because the volcano has become too unstable, too dangerous."

They continued on for a few moments in silence before they stumbled upon yet another scene. This time it showed a wounded griffon lying in the grass, defended by armored giants. The figures held the tips of their spears upwards as a green dragon crashed down upon them. Smoke billowed from a ruined castle in the background. At first, Gwendolyn assumed it was Ballan á Moor. However, when she looked more closely, she realized that the castle could not have been her home. It was much too small—and built well away from the cliffs on which Ballan á Moor sat. The scene shifted once more, and the children saw giants and men building a castle together. Though it was unfinished, they both recognized the beginnings of what was now home.

Gwendolyn pointed to the image of the first castle in ruins. "What is that place?"

Polonius held up his torch and studied the mosaic. "That was Childeric's Keep before Cynder destroyed it."

"Why change locations?" wondered Gwendolyn. "Why not simply rebuild on the old site?"

"With the trolls in the mountains nearby, Childeric chose to build Ballan á Moor in a more defensible place," explained the old man. "As you can see, the cliffs act as a natural barrier." He glanced at the children. "Now come along, we're almost there." Gwendolyn and Polonius continued down the tunnel, but Aethelred stood staring up at the image, lost in thought. Suddenly, he looked around and realized that he was being left behind. "Wait for me," he said, running after them.

On and on they went. Though the shadows of the tunnel gradually yielded to Polonius's torchlight, the journey seemed endless. Finally, they came to a place where the tunnel split into two different directions. The right passageway, which led away east, was a bit smaller than the Low Road which continued straight ahead.

Gwendolyn looked at him expectantly. "Which way?"

"Both lead to the catacombs," explained Polonius. "However, if we continue to follow the path we're on now—the Low Road—we'll find the way blocked thanks to your father and his stone masons. Remember, he had the way in and out sealed years ago—at least, most of the entrances."

Gwendolyn nodded. "To the right then."

Before she took a step, however, her brother asked for a brief rest. "Please," he begged. "We've been walking for hours."

Polonius agreed. The children leaned against the wall and refreshed themselves by taking long drinks from their waterskins. "How long will it take us to reach the catacombs using the smaller tunnel?" asked Aethelred.

At first Polonius didn't respond. Gwendolyn noticed that her tutor continued to hold up the torch as he stared down the Low Road. "Polonius?"

"What? Oh, we're very close now," he replied, as if hearing the children for the first time. "We must be almost underneath the castle. It's just that . . . now that I think about it . . . I don't remember the Low Road extending this far north. I'm going up ahead to get a closer view. Stay here."

Aethelred looked up in surprise. "You're leaving us?"

"No, no," Polonius reassured them. "I won't go far." The children watched the torchlight grow smaller and smaller as he made his way down the long, straight path. Then he stopped for a moment and raised the torch, examining the way ahead. At the edges of the light, he could see piles of stone and earth in the middle of the tunnel that looked like they had been recently disturbed. Polonius walked back to the children quickly.

"We must have made better time than I realized," he said. "Up ahead is the part of the Low Road that your father had sealed. It lies directly below the castle. Only, the wall is no longer there. Someone—or something— has broken through."

As he finished speaking, Gwendolyn heard a noise come from that direction. It was faint but she could clearly hear the sound of metal against metal—or metal on stone. She wasn't sure. Polonius and Aethelred heard it too. The old man put his fingers to his lips. Then he advanced, followed by the children. After a moment, they could hear something else—deep, ugly voices that did not sound like men's. The children had never heard these sounds before, but Polonius had. His face turned pale, and Gwendolyn could see fear in his eyes.

"Trolls," he whispered, shielding the torch with one of his large hands. "Step lightly now and follow me."

Gwendolyn wanted to ask more questions but she knew that it was too great a risk. Polonius continued down the Low Road toward the voices and strange sounds. Was the old man mad? Why weren't they running away? She looked at Aethelred and saw the same confusion in his eyes. If they turned back now, however, they would be alone in the dark. Polonius was the only one among them with torchlight. They could not call out to him nor could they remain behind. They had no choice but to follow him. Gwendolyn swallowed hard and grabbed Aethelred's hand. She hoped Polonius knew what he was doing.

Soon, they were walking past large chunks of rock and earth that had once formed a barrier, but now lay scattered across the tunnel. After a moment the Low Road curved sharply to the right and they saw the flicker of firelight on the opposite wall. Polonius extinguished his torch and crept closer, followed by the children.

When they all peeked around the corner, what Gwendolyn saw seemed strangely familiar. A huge cavern, illuminated by just a few torches, stretched away in front of her. In the shadows, scores of trolls worked feverishly, using picks, shovels, and carts to haul away dirt and loose rock. She had seen drawings of these grotesque creatures before, but it was quite another thing to know they were only a few yards away. They were almost as big as giants, standing twice as tall and broad as a man. However, unlike the giants, they had greasy, tangled hair, scaly skin, and long, yellow nails.

Based on the amount of earth that had removed, Gwendolyn estimated that they must have been digging under the foundations of Ballan á Moor for months. She shuddered. How many nights had she and her family slept soundly while these creatures burrowed under the walls? It was just a matter of time before they emerged through the stone floor and attacked. Then she looked at the castle's foundations above and realized something was wrong. They were not digging up—but down. Suddenly, she understood. They were not attempting to reach the castle at all. Instead, they were searching for a way into the catacombs. That meant they must be searching for the dragon seed. It was the only reasonable explanation. But why now?

Polonius tapped each of the children on the shoulder and motioned for them to come away. After quickly rekindling his torch, he led them back to the place where the Low Road met the smaller tunnel. "This changes things," he said, stopping and rubbing his forehead. "We can no longer reach the catacombs."

"But if the trolls find the seed —" began Gwendolyn.

The old man looked more haggard than ever. "I don't want to imagine what they would do with such power."

"What about this tunnel?" asked Aethelred quietly, pointing down the smaller passageway. "I thought you said we could use it to reach the catacombs?"

"We can," admitted Polonius. "However, it simply leads back to the same place where the trolls are digging, just from a different direction."

"So that's it?" said Aethelred. "We just go back the way we came?"

The old man shook his head. "If we continue down this smaller tunnel, we'll come to an intersection that goes from east to west," he explained. "If we travel west, we'll reach the catacombs—and the trolls."

Aethelred suddenly looked very interested. "And the other direction? That would lead east, correct?"

"By definition," said Polonius. "Unfortunately, that would take us away from the castle and the catacombs— and the seed of Destiny."

"Toward Childeric's Keep?" responded the boy.

"I suppose so." Polonius sighed in exasperation. "Why do you ask?"

Aethelred smiled. "Perhaps we don't have to sneak past the trolls, after all," he said. "If I'm right, they're digging in the *wrong* place."

9

SIGHTLESS EYES

"What are you talking about?" Gwendolyn and Polonius asked at the same time.

Aethelred smiled more broadly, enjoying the momentary confusion of his tutor and sister. The solution was so clear in his mind. Why couldn't they see it? He leaned against the wall and crossed his arms. "Childeric's Keep was destroyed only after Childeric found the dragon seed, correct?"

"Yes," replied Polonius, annoyed with the boy's seemingly irrelevant questions. "We don't have time for history lessons now, Aethelred. What is your point?"

"Then I'll get right to it," he explained. "I think Childeric hid the seed there, long before Ballan á Moor was built."

"Why would he do that?" asked Gwendolyn.

"Don't you see?" said Aethelred impatiently. "If Childeric took the seed, he must have hidden it before the dragon attacked, for there are no records of it being seen again. Where else would it be if not the Keep?"

"That's just speculation," declared Polonius. "People have been looking for the seed of Destiny for years.

Don't you think they would have picked over the ruins of Childeric's Keep long ago?"

"Perhaps," admitted Aethelred. "Or perhaps the reason why Childeric chose to build the catacombs underneath Ballan á Moor was to make people *believe* he had hidden it there."

Gwendolyn smirked. "Wouldn't it make more sense to simply hide it in the catacombs?"

Aethelred, however, never doubted himself. "Only if Childeric had possession of it."

"I'm so confused," muttered Gwendolyn, holding her head.

Aethelred ignored her. "Why don't we ever hear of people seeing the seed after Childeric stole it?" He turned to Polonius. "Why didn't Edubard know where it was? Doesn't that seem strange to you?"

"I'm afraid I agree with Gwendolyn," stated Polonius. "It would be much wiser to hide it in a place like the catacombs. If the seed lies among the ruins of Childeric's Keep, it would mean it is virtually unguarded."

Aethelred smiled again. "Unguarded, but not *unprotected*," he replied. "Remember the first stanza of Childeric's Riddle:

If you wish to seek my prize,
disturb its rest and cause its rise
Think you twice, for deep it lies
under a ring of sightless eyes.

The boy looked at his sister. "Gwen, you've spent a lot of time among the ruins. Isn't there a well there?"

"Yes," she admitted, remembering an old well that had been boarded up ever since she could remember. "But what does that have to do with anything?"

"The well is surrounded by large stone columns?" he continued.

Gwendolyn began to grow impatient again. "So what?"

"Rectangular columns, right?" he hinted. "All shaped like a certain *letter*?"

Polonius chuckled. "I think I see," he said. "'The phrase in the riddle—sightless eyes—can also mean *sightless I's*, like the letter. Is that what you mean, Aethelred?"

The boy nodded, grinning from ear to ear. "Don't you see, Gwen? Each of the columns that surround the well looks like a capital I. Together they form a ring. A ring of sightless I's."

"Clever," Gwendolyn acknowledged. "However, the riddle says *under* a ring, doesn't it?"

Aethelred agreed. "He must have hidden it down the well."

Gwendolyn and Polonius looked at one another. Though neither wanted to admit it, Aethelred's guess sounded more plausible than they had originally thought. It was certainly much better than returning to the Low Road with trolls so near.

"I suppose we have little choice," replied Polonius at last. "If we try to enter the catacombs, it will just be a matter of time before we are discovered by the trolls. Come along."

While not nearly as large or ornate as the Low Road, the tunnel in which they now traveled was straight and flat, allowing the three of them to make good progress.

Not for the last time, Gwendolyn and Aethelred were glad that Polonius had made them pack some food before leaving camp. They ate and drank as they walked, munching on biscuits and dried sausage. As usual, Polonius led the way, softly humming a strange tune that the children had never heard before. Soon they came to the intersection that he had described. They turned the corner and continued walking east. However, they had only walked a short time more when Polonius stopped and held up his hand.

"What is it?" asked Gwendolyn, finishing her biscuit.

The old man wrinkled his nose. "Don't you smell it?" he responded. "The air is salty."

Using the torchlight, he examined the red tiles that covered the walls on either side. The torch illuminated what they might have otherwise missed—stone rungs leading upwards to a smaller hole in the ceiling. "I suspect that leads above ground," he explained. At the top, about twenty feet above them, the rungs disappeared into another smaller opening.

"Shall I go first?" inquired the old man.

"I'll go if you don't mind," said Aethelred, bothered by the thought of remaining in the tunnels without Polonius. He turned to his sister. "That is, if you'll be right behind me, Gwen."

Gwendolyn nodded. "Lead the way."

When the children reached the top, they continued to follow the rungs that led into the hole in the ceiling. Polonius followed carefully from behind. Though this passage was much narrower than the tunnel, they found the going easy. Soon, they felt cold, salty air coming from the darkness above. The next moment, they could see light ahead. Finally, Polonius and the children emerged from a crack in what looked like the floor of a narrow cave. They stood up in the dim light and surveyed their surroundings. With the exception of a few bats that fluttered overhead, the place was unoccupied. Polonius extinguished the torch and led the children out of the cave, pushing aside the bushes that concealed the entrance.

Once their eyes had adjusted to the early morning sunlight, they recognized the area almost immediately. Rolling green hills spread out before them, with large stones poking out of the tall grass in the distance. A flock of seagulls circled in the air high above. The sea was a short distance away. Not far from where they stood, the three could clearly see the stone ruins of a castle.

"Childeric's Keep," said Gwendolyn. "Well done, Polonius."

The old man looked puzzled. "I had no idea this entrance was here." He didn't have time to ponder this discovery, however, for Gwendolyn and Aethelred were already running through the tall grass to the site of the ruin. Gwendolyn was very familiar with this place. Large slabs of bleached stone lay here and there, crumbling and abandoned, while weeds and wild flowers had long since conquered the fragments of cobblestone under their feet. The shaft of the well, also in need of repair, was surrounded by six stone columns that had once supported a dome. Over time, someone had covered the mouth of the well with thick planks of wood to prevent accidents.

"You see!" shouted Aethelred, pointing to the circular mouth of the well. "This must be the ring in Childeric's riddle." He motioned to the stone columns. "And these, of course, are the sightless I's."

Gwendolyn eyed the boards that covered the well's mouth. "Can you help us remove these, Polonius?"

The old man's axe made quick work of the planks. The children peered down into the darkness of the well, wondering what lay at the bottom. As they suspected, however, they could see nothing. Gwendolyn even dropped a pebble over the edge but heard no splash.

"A clever interpretation of Childeric's riddle, Aethelred, I'll grant you," said the old man, finally. "But what are we to do now?"

Gwendolyn's eyes brightened. "Do you have a rope in your pack?"

"Yes," he replied, confused. "What—wait! You don't think you're going down there, do you?"

"Why not?" she demanded. "You're too big to fit."

Polonius flared his nostrils. "First, it will be too dark to see anything, my dear."

"Your torch —" she began.

"Won't work if it's wet," he replied. Then he leaned over and gazed into the well. "Speaking of which, that water must be very cold. You'd freeze to death. Perhaps most important, if the rhyme is true, this abyss is guarded by *a thing unseen*, remember? I won't have you risking your life."

Gwendolyn glared at him. "What would you have us do?" she muttered. "Continue to stay out here in the open with Destiny on the loose? We don't have time to play it safe, Polonius! Besides, if you lower me down, all I have to do is give a shout or tug on the rope, and you can pull me back up. I just want to take a look around."

The old man stroked his beard. "I don't know," he said, doubtfully. "If something were to happen to you, Gwendolyn, I couldn't bear it. Your father would have my head if he thought I was even considered letting you go down a well alone."

"None of us may have heads once the Merovians arrive," she replied.

The old man struggled to come up with a sound argument, but could not refute her logic. These were desperate times. "Very well," he conceded. "You can look, but you're only likely to find old well water. I insist, however, on pulling you up after only a minute—and less than that if I feel you tug at the rope."

Gwendolyn agreed. She handed her sword and the rest of her things to Aethelred who hadn't said a word since she suggested exploring the well. "Don't worry," she said, smiling. "I'm just going to take a look around."

He nodded reluctantly. "Just don't do anything . . . too brave."

Polonius found his rope and made sure the knot was tight with a loop for Gwendolyn to sit on before he allowed her to approach the well's edge. Then, handing her the rekindled torch, he lowered her down the well. Aethelred and Polonius both watched anxiously as she disappeared into the void. The old man continued to lower her slowly, hand over hand, down into the darkness. Soon, they could only see the torchlight flickering faintly far below.

Aethelred leaned over the well and held his hands up to his mouth. "What do you see, Gwen?"

"Just the sides of the well," came the reply, echoing out of the darkness. "There's still no water. Let me down a bit more."

Polonius sighed but continued to give the rope slack. After a moment more, however, he noticed that half of the rope's length was now beyond the edge of the well.

"She must have reached the water by now," he said, puzzled. "We're too near the sea for the water table to be any deeper."

"How long is the rope?" asked Aethelred.

"A hundred feet," responded the old man. "I will not risk going any lower."

Before he tightened his grip, however, Polonius felt the rope jerk violently. "Gwendolyn!" he cried, hauling the rope up as quickly as he could. "Gwendolyn!" The rope's weightlessness confirmed his fear before he saw the other end.

Gwendolyn had disappeared.

***

Polonius and Aethelred continued to shout Gwendolyn's name into the darkness. No answer came. They were frantic with worry and also confused by the way in which she had vanished. Why had she not cried out? Aethelred begged Polonius to lower him down into the well to search for his sister (which was quite a brave thing for a ten-year old boy to do after Gwendolyn had just disappeared). Polonius, of course, refused.

"If you think I'm going to risk your life too, you're a bigger fool than I am," he scoffed. Normally, Polonius would never have spoken to anyone in such a way, especially a child, but he was half-mad with worry and guilt for having consented to Gwendolyn's plan, and could not think clearly. Nevertheless, his words caused Aethelred's eyes to well up with tears. Polonius sighed deeply and drew the boy close.

"Forgive me, lad," he said, hugging him. "I didn't mean it."

"I know," replied Aethelred, wiping his eyes. "But how else can we reach her?"

"I don't know," the old man responded, close to despair. "If I could rip these stones away to get down there, I would."

Aethelred looked up at him with round eyes. "Perhaps there is another way! The tunnel from which we emerged—in the cave. Where does it lead?"

"I—I don't know," murmured Polonius. "It continued to lead east."

The boy looked up at him. "Then maybe it leads to the other end of the well?"

Polonius gazed down into the darkness of the stone mouth once again. He hated the thought of leaving. What if she called out for help and they were no longer here? However, they should have heard something by now if she were able to speak—and he would go mad if he simply sat and waited. He looked back at Aethelred.

"Very well," he replied. "But we leave the rope here, in case she needs it." He quickly tied one end of the rope to a stone column, and dropped the rest of it down the well. "Hang on, Gwendolyn!" he cried. "We're coming!"

As the two made their way back to the cave, Polonius realized that Gwendolyn had taken the torch with her into the well. They would have no light to guide them when they descended again into the tunnels. He tore some fabric from his cloak and wrapped it around a large branch that he found near one of the bushes that concealed the cave's entrance. Using some of the oil in his pack, he sprinkled it on the fabric, and used his flint to set the torch on fire. Then he led Aethelred back into the cave and down the stone rungs.

They had just reached the bottom of the tunnel when they saw torchlight dimly in the distance. It was accompanied by the soft but unmistakable sound of footsteps approaching in the direction from which they had originally come.

Now that he knew that trolls lurked in the tunnels, Polonius's instinct told him to remain hidden before confirming the identity of the torch's owner. Before he could whisper this to Aethelred, however, the boy ran forward. "Gwendolyn?" he called, desperately. "Gwendolyn!"

The sound of the footsteps stopped. Aethelred, frantic to find his sister, ran ahead, forcing Polonius to follow. What they saw next startled them: a Merovian boy, alone, stood facing them in the darkness.

"Ghael?" said Aethelred, at once confused and disappointed. The other boy (for it was indeed Ghael) held up his torch to see them. His face was streaked with dirt and sweat, but he looked relieved.

"There you are!" cried Ghael, smiling, as if Polonius and Aethelred should have been expecting him. "I've been looking for you." He wore a small pack, with a sword slung across his back.

Polonius frowned, stunned by the boy's presence. "What are you doing here?" he demanded.

"I overheard you talking in the tent," explained Ghael, looking strangely guilty. "I followed you here because you said it wasn't safe in the forest."

Polonius's frown deepened. He was sure that they had escaped the camp undetected. How had the boy followed them all this way without being discovered? Wasn't he supposed to be advising Argus on the Merovian fleet's whereabouts and tactics? What was he doing eavesdropping on the children in camp, anyway? How could he have come so far without being seen by the trolls?

"Perhaps you also remember, then, that you'd be safer if you weren't in Gwendolyn's presence?" grumbled Polonius, angrily. "Besides, the tunnels come with their own dangers, as I'm sure you overheard."

Ghael nodded. "I understand—but Sköll's fleet will be here soon, so the dragon isn't the only thing to worry about is it? Please don't be angry." He wiped the sweat from his face with his forearm and looked confused. "Speaking of Gwendolyn, where is she?" He looked at Aethelred. "Where is your sister?"

"She went down the well in the ruins of Childeric's Keep, and then she just . . . disappeared," said Aethelred, remembering again the urgency with which they sought his sister.

"Disappeared?" replied Ghael, his expression now one of concern. "Why would she go down a well?"

"She was looking for the lost seed of Destiny —" began Aethelred.

Polonius put his hand on the boy's shoulder. "I'll ask the questions here."

Suddenly, deep, guttural sounds filled the tunnel in the direction from which Ghael had just come. They were not, however, human voices. Rather, they were harsh, angry voices. Troll voices.

***

"Follow me!" whispered Polonius.

The old man led the boys east as he held the torch high above his head to light the way. The path was full of twists and turns, but at least it sloped slightly downward, allowing them to move quickly. They ran and ran until the children's breathing became audible. Though they could no longer hear the trolls, Polonius demanded that they keep moving. He wanted to put as much distance between them and the wicked creatures as possible. Finally, Aethelred begged for a brief rest. Polonius handed around a waterskin and the children drank deeply. "I thought the trolls were only digging under Ballan á Moor?" said Aethelred. "What are they doing out here?"

Polonius shook his head wearily. "I don't know." Then he crouched down and leaned forward on his knees to rest his feet. "Perhaps it is no coincidence that the Merovians have chosen to attack even as the trolls burrow into the foundations of the castle," he added. "They may be working together." He rubbed a bead of sweat that trickled from his forehead. "Now there's no question we need the giants' help." Grimstad, however, was far, far away, and as long as Argus remained king, any hope of reconciling with the giants seemed like a dream.

"What now, Polonius?" asked Ghael, studying his face carefully.

The old man rose to his feet. "I will not leave Gwendolyn behind," he vowed. "We must continue to search for her. If she's down here, we'll find her."

"I wish I had never heard of Childeric's Riddle," muttered Aethelred. "It's my fault, you see." He looked up at Polonius, guilty. "It's just my foolish imagination. That well could never have been the seed's resting place. As you said, Polonius, it must be under Ballan á Moor."

Polonius put his hands on the boy's shoulder and looked at him sternly. "Now you listen to me, lad," he said. "I'll not have you blaming yourself for this. It was my decision to let Gwendolyn go down the well. As for your imagination, don't ever apologize for that. It's a gift." Aethelred nodded and looked away.

"Come now," declared the old man. "We must continue to look for your sister."

The tunnel continued to slope downward which meant less work for their legs but it also took them deeper underground. The air was cold and dry now. Suddenly, the passageway intersected with another tunnel. Polonius stopped and stared first in one direction, then the other.

"Which way?" gasped Aethelred. He was breathing hard again and thankful for the rest. Even in the torchlight, Polonius could see that the boy's face was flushed.

"Just a moment," he said. "I must be sure." After a moment, he pointed left. "The right passageway leads east, I believe."

"How do you know?" asked Aethelred.

"It's easy if you can read the ancient language of the giants." Polonius pointed to one of the tiles in the wall a few meters above the boy's head. It bore a symbol that looked like a square encompassed by an incomplete triangle. "That is pronounced *arda*," he explained, "Or, as we would say, east."

"And the left?" inquired Aethelred. He noticed another stone, with a different symbol, embedded into the wall in that direction. The image looked like an anvil above a crescent moon. "That leads west?"

Polonius nodded. "Yes, back to the mountains—and Ozzo's Furnace."

Aethelred looked around. "Where's Ghael?"

Polonius looked back down the way from which they had come. The boy was gone. "He was right behind me a moment ago. When did you last see him?"

"Not less than a minute ago," replied Aethelred, his eyes growing wider. "Do you think the trolls—"

"Of course not!" stated Polonius, trying to assuage the boy's fear. Trolls were not subtle creatures, and would have attacked them openly if they had greater numbers. Then a new thought troubled Polonius. What if there was only one troll? A scout, perhaps, that couldn't resist snatching one of the boys from behind? If so, there was no time to lose. "Am I to lose every child in my charge?" Polonius thought to himself. He glanced back at the direction from which they had come. "I'm going after him."

"But the trolls —" began Aethelred.

"Let me worry about the trolls!" Polonius snapped. "You must stay here. I can move much faster without you."

"You have the torch!" the boy pleaded. "I will be all alone in the darkness!"

"No, you won't," said Polonius, handing the boy the torch. While trolls can see very well in the dark compared to giants, Polonius could still do well enough underground, relying upon his hearing and his sense of smell to guide him.

"Polonius!" cried Aethelred, too frightened to be ashamed of the fear he now felt. "I'm afraid."

Polonius was about to scold the boy again but he relented. Aethelred had been walking for hours. It would be a great deal to ask a grown man to navigate strange tunnels with trolls lurking about. It must be even harder for a ten-year old boy. Polonius reached down and cupped Aethelred's chin in one of his great hands. "Do not be afraid, Aethelred," he said softly. "The blood of kings flows in your veins. You are stronger than you perhaps yet realize." A few tears ran down the boy's cheeks as he gazed steadily at his tutor. Polonius hated to do this but he couldn't simply abandon Ghael to the trolls. "I will return—I promise you. However, you must stay here. Do you hear me? Stay right *here*."

Aethelred nodded his head and wiped away his tears. Polonius nodded, patted him on the shoulder, and then ran back up the tunnel. In a moment, Aethelred was all alone as the torch flickered weakly in his hand.

10

A POWER UNSEEN

When Polonius had lowered Gwendolyn into the mouth of the well, all she could see was the mossy stone walls that the torch revealed around her. However, the firelight could not penetrate the darkness beneath her. She simply had to wait, sitting uncomfortably across the thick rope, as she descended a little at a time.

Gwendolyn fully expected to feel cold water on her feet at any moment. Despite going deeper and deeper underground, however, she felt nothing. When Aethelred shouted to her, asking what she saw, she had responded truthfully. There was no water. No anything, really—just the curved, stone walls of the well. No sooner had she spoken, when everything suddenly changed.

As she descended lower, the narrow confines of the well abruptly disappeared. Gwendolyn clutched the rope tightly and looked around. She hung suspended, like a spider at the end of its web, over a tremendous void. Peering into the shadows, she tried to comprehend the enormity of the cavern in which she now found herself. Its rocky walls did not seem to be made by human or even giant hands. It was instead one of nature's marvels, the likes of which even our world still possesses, as if to remind us that beauty and terror are sometimes related.

Gwendolyn shifted her weight, careful to keep the torch away from the rope, as Polonius continued to lower her down. The cavern, she realized in awe, spanned hundreds of feet in diameter, held together by nothing more than a fortuitous assembly of stone and earth. Or at least so it seemed to her. Even more mysterious, however, was the light. She realized that the torch she carried was no longer necessary. Far below shimmered a green pool whose reflection danced on the walls around her.

"The abyss of ghostly green . . ." she said, remembering Childeric's Riddle. "Aethelred was right."

She was about to call out to Polonius and her brother when she saw the source of the green light. Submerged deep in the center of the pool, surrounded by large stones, shone a smooth, round object. Though still hanging from the rope far above, she knew it immediately to be the seed. Its warmth and its power called out to her. However, she also felt something more—an intelligence and a will that resided within it that were unique. As if in response to her presence, it sparkled brightly, illuminating the cavern with hard, green light.

Gwendolyn caught her breath. "What Edubard would have given for this discovery!" she whispered. "How much more powerful would he have been if he could have put his hands on it, possessing the full measure of its magic?" Now the seed lay before her, just a few hundred feet away, glowing in power and might. Her father might be too afraid to use the seed's power—too afraid to even acknowledge its existence—and yet here it

was! Hers foi
father's weakne
on the wretchec
on the giants, wi
Destiny herself!
Gwendolyn the Gi

Roy Sakelson

prepared Gwendolyn for the
her dive caused her to g
when she emerged s
water's temperatu
Gasping and s
seed. Ther
what w
poc

Then, quite un
emotion, one of pity
as her desire to wiei
help but feel sorry for
and for how its powei
Childeric and Edubare   the
dragon if she were to c   magic from it?
Would it die? Or was it   to remain in its shell
forever, a prisoner of her desire? Irritated, she pushed
this thought away. Was she becoming as weak as her
father? The power to defeat Valmar's enemies lay before
her, and she was concerned about a dragon's life? This
was no time to be sentimental. What was a dragon's life,
when so many other lives hung in the balance?

Gwendolyn knew what she must do. Even if Polonius
agreed to allow her to reach the seed, the rope was much
too short to lower her safely down. But there was
another way. She hoped Polonius and Aethelred would
understand why she chose not to tell them what she was
about to do—but their approval was not necessary. She
dropped the torch. She no longer needed it; the green
light showed her the way down. With a splash and a hiss
it sunk into the pool below. Using the rope, she pulled
herself up until her right foot rested on the loop. Then,
judging the water deep enough, she let go.

She hit the surface with a great splash. Despite being
an excellent swimmer, however, nothing could have

water's chill. The height of
deep below the surface, and
still felt out of breath, for the
had caused her chest to tighten.
uttering, she paddled her way toward the
she realized that even if she could reach it,
uld she do with it? It was at the bottom of the
. How could she ever lift it? No matter. She just
needed to touch it. That would solve things, somehow.
Perhaps she could draw more of its power, more of its
warmth. Soon, she would be invincible.

Suddenly, the green light, once bright, began to fade.
She swam nearer to the seed, but it continued to grow
dimmer. "No!" she cried. "Wait!"

In a matter of seconds, the light went out, and
plunged the cavern—and Gwendolyn—into darkness.

***

Gwendolyn felt more afraid and more alone than at
any other time in her short life. The cold water literally
took her breath away, and she found it difficult to breath.
Even worse, she felt helpless. She cursed her poor
judgment. Why had she jumped into the pool without
telling Polonius and Aethelred? Save for reaching the
seed, she had no plan whatsoever. Now she found
herself freezing to death. Already, her fingers and toes
were going numb. She continued to tread water without
any idea of how to reach safety.

Perhaps the only good thing that had come of her
rashness was that she was so angry at her stupidity that
she refused to feel sorry for herself. She thought of
testing the depth of the water, hoping to find part of it

shallow enough in which to stand. After diving several times, she abandoned the idea when she realized she could not hold her breath in the cold water for even a short amount of time. The only choice was to swim for the sides, and hope to find a ledge or at least an outcropping of rock that would allow her to hang on.

Where were the edges of the pool? In the darkness that surrounded her, she had lost all sense of direction. She couldn't afford to lose any more time in the cold water. "Think!" she told herself. Remembering what she could of the cavern's dimensions, she recalled that the closest edge lay behind her. She still wasn't sure which way would be the shortest, or if there would be any ledge to hold when she got there, but she had no other choice.

To distract herself from the cold, she thought of the words of Childeric's Riddle. What were they again? Something about a ghostly abyss, which she now understood all too well. What came next? She tried to recall the words, but her teeth were chattering, make it hard to concentrate. Then she remembered.

In an abyss of ghostly green
it rests though restless as it dreams,
Guarded by a power unseen
you must defeat to be redeemed.

Guarded by a power *unseen*? That could be anything in this darkness! Why did her great grandfather create such a maddening riddle? Perhaps that's why some called it *Childeric's Curse*, she thought grimly. The last thing one does in this abyss is *curse* his name.

Another thought occurred to her. *A power unseen.* Her power! If she could conjure it perhaps she could save herself? The last time she had felt the magic flow through her body, Destiny was attacking her, while threatening her brother's life. Gwendolyn remembered the fear and anger that had welled up inside of her like lava from a dormant volcano. But though she felt anger now, too, it was a cold, self-reproachful anger. It was not born out of passion to save Aethelred, but out of greed—greed for the seed's power.

Then her outstretched hands, now clumsy from the cold, felt something hard and rough. She must have reached the perimeter of the cavern! She felt wildly, searching for something to grab, anything that would allow her to rest for a moment. However, she only felt the smooth, wet edges of rock that slanted upwards. She swam first to the left, then to the right, splashing in the darkness, searching in vain for a hold. Already her legs were becoming numb, and she knew she had perhaps a minute or two before they would stop working, exhausted. Death would quickly follow.

Close to despair, a final thought came to her in the darkness. Perhaps with her death in this cavern, the dragon's power that resided in her would flow back to its source, back to the seed that lay at the bottom of these strange waters. She would have liked to make peace between Valmar and the Western Giants. But the power that she inherited had never really belonged to her, she realized with shame—never belonged to her ancestors, the giants, or the trolls who sought its power. It belonged only to the dragon for which it had been naturally intended. It was true that she could not control the circumstances through which she had inherited the seed's extraordinary power. She could, however, control the decisions that made her want to abuse the dragon magic.

That ability to choose, she realized, was in some ways the most powerful magic of all.

Gwendolyn tried to move her arms and legs but they no longer responded. She was completely numb. As she sank into the dark water, she felt the pool's cold, deadly embrace. The last thing she saw was a dim, green light flickering somewhere below.

***

Aethelred stood perfectly still, not knowing what to do. Alone deep underground, he did not feel at all brave. Why had Gwendolyn insisted on going down the well alone? Why had Ghael disappeared? If the boy was playing tricks, Aethelred vowed that he would knock him down when Polonius caught up to him and brought him back. And Polonius! How could he just leave him here?

His eyes shifted from the direction Polonius had fled and turned to the winding tunnel before him. The torchlight showed his surroundings well enough. Curved, tiled walls seemed to stretch forever onward but they provided little warmth. Now that he had stopped walking, he felt the chill and dampness more keenly. He also felt hungry, and recalled wistfully the last proper meal he had had while back in camp. Then he remembered the sausage and apples he carried. Leaning the torch carefully against the wall, he dug into his pack and pulled out an apple.

After a few bites, however, he saw a dull light coming from up ahead. Aethelred stopped chewing, his cheeks bulging with apple, as he peered up the passageway. What could it be? Another torch? Polonius had gone in the opposite direction. Perhaps trolls were coming to get him. This light, however, lacked the warm, orange glow of fire. Instead, it was green. Did trolls use green fire?

The light grew stronger. Perhaps it was a troll after all? Or a dozen. What if even now they were simply right around the corner, waiting for him to fall asleep? No, thought Aethelred bleakly. Trolls would not need to surprise him. They would simply chase him until they caught him. He imagined the long, green legs outpacing him in a matter of seconds. He wondered what it would be like to feel the beast's firm grip, its sharp teeth, yellow eyes, and the stink of its breath as it drew close to him. The thought made him feel sick. "Polonius may say that my imagination is a gift, but sometimes it sure doesn't feel like it," he grumbled.

Then Aethelred surprised himself. "Perhaps I'm not as brave as my sister, but I'm tired of imagining what's out there," he said. "If this thing is going to play hide and seek with me, I may as well see what it is!" He swallowed hard, dropped the apple, and stood up. Gripping his torch in one hand and his blade in the other, he made his way toward the light. He walked slowly at first, thrusting the torch out before him. Then he was comforted when he remembered that trolls didn't especially like fire, using it only when necessary. "If they attack me, I'll give them a good burn they won't soon forget!"

He quickened his pace and rounded the corner. What he saw next made him gasp. The tunnel opened into a vast cavern. In front of him, just a few feet away, was a large, underground pool illuminated by a green light. Trying to identify the source of the light, he approached the edge of the water. He saw a person floating just underneath the surface. His eyes widened in alarm as he let go of his torch and his sword. "Gwen?"

He dropped to his stomach and reached his arm out as far as it could go. He just managed to grab her leg. It was limp. In fact, she wasn't moving at all. Trying not to panic, he grabbed her other leg and dragged her closer to him. Then, taking her by the arms, he pulled her torso over the pool's rough, stony edge, his muscles straining against her dead weight. He quickly pulled the rest of her body to safety. He kneeled over her, cradling her head gently in his lap, and brushed the wet hair out of her face. Her skin was cold—too cold. "Gwendolyn!" he said again. She didn't respond.

His heart began to beat rapidly. How long had she been in the pool? Was she dead? Fear began to consume him when suddenly she coughed up water. Then her eyes fluttered open and looked up at him.

"You're alive!" he cried.

She nodded and smiled faintly, still weak from her experience. "Well," she said, her eyes twinkling. "You were right."

"What do you mean?" he asked, looking at the vast pool before him, then back to his sister.

"Childeric's Riddle," she replied, putting her hand into his and squeezing it gently. "You solved it."

When Gwendolyn had regained some of her strength, Aethelred helped her squeeze the water from her dress, and gave her some of the food he carried. As she ate, they shared their experiences, marveling at all that had happened in such a short amount of time. Finally, Aethelred helped her to her feet. She looked at him proudly as he turned to gaze across the pool, which continued to glow a faint green.

"After all this time," he said, ruefully. "Here lies the seed of Destiny."

"I don't fully understand it yet, Aeth," she admitted. "However, I think that when the seed realized I intended to rob it of its power, it hid its light from me."

He looked skeptical. "But it was shining brightly when I found you," he said, as he watched the pool's reflection dance on the cavern walls. "Just as it's shining now."

She nodded softly. "Only after I realized that my intentions were selfish, and that it's wrong to want to use the dragon magic that our great-grandfather stole," she answered. "By the time I realized it, however, it must have been too late. I could no longer feel my limbs." She looked at him and smiled. "You saved my life."

Aethelred smiled back at his sister. "If that's the case, then you had as much to do with it as I did. If the light had not reappeared, I wouldn't have found you." Suddenly, his eyes brightened. "I think I understand. Remember the words in Childeric's Riddle? 'The seed is guarded by a power unseen you must defeat to be redeemed.' You *defeated* the power. You *passed* the test."

Now it was Gwendolyn's turn to look skeptical. "I didn't defeat anything!"

"Of course you did," replied Aethelred. "You defeated your desire for more power—to use the seed in a way that would make you stronger but only at the expense of the seed itself."

"I never thought of it that way before," she said, impressed by her brother's insight.

His smile broadened. "Sometimes it's easier to see clearly only after the danger has passed."

"The danger is far from passed, Aeth," she warned. "Others still seek its power. You must promise me that we'll keep this place a secret. No one must be able to exploit the dragon seed."

"As you wish," he responded. "I suppose, however, that if I were born with the power, as you were, it would be more difficult for me to agree to protect the seed."

"No," objected Gwendolyn. "It would be easier. For once you understand that the seed is not an object—but a living thing—you cannot help but feel a kinship with it."

"What I can't understand is how the seed has remained undisturbed here for so long," he wondered, gazing down upon the glowing object. "Though this tunnel appears to be the only entrance to the cavern— save for the well entrance above—surely the giants must have discovered this when they dug the passageway?"

"I'm sure of it," replied Gwendolyn. "However, as I just experienced a short while ago, it can remain hidden if it chooses, quickly dimming its light. A dark seed at the bottom of a dark lake is not easily found. You'd have to know exactly what you were looking for."

Aethelred agreed. "What's to become of it now?"

Gwendolyn looked at her brother, puzzled. "What do you mean?"

"Well, if we keep it a secret, is it to stay here forever?"

"You think that it should be given the opportunity to hatch?" she asked.

"I didn't say that," he corrected her. "I've seen the damage a dragon can do. Why would we risk dealing with another such beast when Destiny already threatens Valmar?"

"What if this one's different?" she asked, with a strange look in her eye.

"What if it's not?" he replied, doubtfully, before glancing at her. "Are you willing to take that risk?"

Gwendolyn didn't answer. Instead, she gazed intently at the pool. "I suppose it makes little difference. Remember what Polonius told us. The only way for a dragon's seed to hatch is by dragon's fire." But even as she said these words, she thought it deserved the chance to be born—the chance to live. She felt somehow that this dragon was different from the rest. "Oh, I wish Polonius were here. He'd know what to do."

As she spoke those words, the children heard the sound of footsteps approaching.

"At last, Polonius has returned," said Aethelred, joyfully. The boy began walking up the curved tunnel, still holding his torch and his sword. "I've found her, Polonius! I found Gwendolyn! Did you find Ghael? I hope he wasn't playing games."

For reasons she could not explain, Gwendolyn had a horrible feeling in the pit of her stomach. "Wait, Aethelred," she whispered, catching up to him and trying to stop him from going forward. "It's not safe." As she did so, the pool's green light began to fade. Just as she put her hand on her brother's shoulder, however, she saw what she had feared. Four large trolls turned the corner with scimitars drawn.

The leader smiled at the children wickedly. "There you are!" he growled. "Just where he said you'd be!"

At that moment, the green light beneath the pool disappeared, and the children were left staring at the trolls in the dim torchlight.

11

BEHIND THE MASK

Aethelred screamed as one of the trolls lunged forward and tried to grab him. Trolls were not known for being very quick, but underground, where there was not much room to maneuver, their great strength and ability to see in the dark were more than enough to overwhelm most enemies. Aethelred, to his credit, never gave up. He fought back with a fury that Gwendolyn had never before seen, slashing at the air in front of him with both his sword and his torch which kept the creature momentarily at bay. Sensing the boy's inexperience, however, the troll deflected Aethelred's sword and then kicked him savagely in the chest. The blow sent Aethelred sprawling backwards as his weapon and the torch both fell to the floor. The next moment, the troll was upon him.

Seeing her brother struggle in the creature's grasp, Gwendolyn forgot her fear. Retrieving both the sword and the torch, she charged Aethelred's captor, waving her blade wildly. "Put him down!" she screamed. Before she could take another step, however, another troll grabbed her sword arm from behind, twisting it painfully until she dropped her weapon.

"Girls shouldn't play with swords," he grunted, leaning down over her shoulder. "You could get hurt."

Unfortunately for the troll, Gwendolyn still held the torch. Thinking fast, she thrust the flaming tip over her shoulder and into the creature's eye. He howled in pain and knocked the torch out of her hands before clutching his face and staggering backwards. The smell of scorched flesh filled the air. Suddenly, the torch's flame sputtered and died, plunging everything into darkness.

"Aethelred! Where are you?" she cried, groping blindly for her brother. Even as she did so, however, she felt a sharp blow to her head, and fell to the floor, unconscious. Aethelred continued to struggle, but could do nothing against the troll's strength.

"Ha!" laughed one of the creatures. "That little mouse took your eye, Bogg!"

"She did, indeed," snickered the troll that held Aethelred. "Did you hear how Bogg screamed?" The others seemed to enjoy their companion's misery.

"Give her to me!" snarled Bogg, still clutching his face. "I'll teach *her* how to use fire!" He stumbled toward Gwendolyn, intent on killing her.

"No!" shouted the leader, who was larger and more evil looking than the others. His name was Gimlash. Both of his large nostrils were pierced by silver rings, and the scars across his chest revealed that he was no stranger to violence. It was he who had smiled at the children when the trolls appeared. "I've already given her a knock she'll feel when she wakes," he barked. "That's enough for now." He looked around the cavern. "Where is the man?" Then, he leaned down and came face to face with Aethelred, who was still held tightly by another troll. Gimlash, like his companions, could see perfectly well in the dark. He enjoyed watching the boy's frightened eyes searching blindly in the darkness.

"Where is the man that was with you?" said the troll, grabbing Aethelred's face with one of his calloused hands. Fortunately, the boy could not see the troll's hideous features. The creature's face was so close, however, that he could smell Gimlash's rotten breath and feel the spittle that escaped his mouth.

"I don't know!" whimpered Aethelred.

Gimlash snorted before narrowing his eyes. "No matter," he said. "We have what we need." He looked across the pool that lay at his feet. "At least half of it."

"What about my eye?" whined Bogg.

"It's a good thing you have *another* one, isn't it?" sneered Gimlash. "Now hold them fast until I return— they are not to be harmed. Do you understand? The seed must be in the pool."

Though he could still see nothing, Aethelred heard a splash, and guessed that the leader must have gone into the water. Gimlash's night vision made it easy for him to search the bottom. It took him less than a minute. When the troll surfaced again, he produced a large stone and lifted it out of the water, gently setting it on the ground. The stone did not sparkle as it had for Gwendolyn. It now merely looked like a large rock. The other trolls stared at it stupidly, doubtful of its worth.

"That doesn't look like a dragon seed," said one.

"I may have lost my eye," sneered Bogg. "But you've lost your mind, Gimlash, if you think that's worth anything. I can see hundreds of stones just like it at the bottom of this pool from where I stand." The other two trolls nodded their heads in agreement.

Gimlash climbed out of the water and stood before them. "Fools! You need only touch it to understand."

Bogg reached forward and put a large hand on the seed. "It's warm!" he said, astonished.

"Of course it is!" spat Gimlash. "It is the lost seed of Destiny. Soon, he will use its power to give us what we have so long sought!"

"Revenge!" shouted the others, licking their lips.

Gimlash picked up the seed while the other bound Gwendolyn and Aethelred with coarse rope. Then, carrying the children, the trolls marched back up the tunnel from which they had come.

***

With Gwendolyn still unconscious, poor Aethelred had to endure the darkness of the tunnels, the rough handling of the trolls, and the horrible feeling of being helpless in their grasp—alone. He tried to keep up his courage, whispering to his sister, hoping she would respond. "Gwendolyn?" he whispered. "Please wake up. Gwendolyn, can you hear me?" There was no answer. In fact, in the pitch darkness, he didn't even know if she was still in his company. It was a difficult time. He couldn't help but imagine the terrible plans his captors had for him. Nevertheless, he continued to whisper his sister's name, repeating it over and over again desperately.

Finally, Gwendolyn regained consciousness and heard her brother's words. "I'm here, Aeth," she said in a small voice. Her head throbbed as she remembered the trolls' hideous faces, and wished she had not given them an advantage by using the torch so recklessly. She was grateful, however, that her brother was still with her. "What's happening?" she asked.

Aethelred's heart leaped at the sound of her voice. "They're taking us somewhere," he replied, "and they have the seed."

"No more talking!" growled Gimlash. "Or maybe I will let Bogg pay you back!"

Gwendolyn was crushed. Just as she had discovered the seed, it had been taken from her. She had pledged to be its guardian—and she had failed. She hung her head in the darkness, exhausted, and didn't say another word. Other than an occasional grunt, the trolls made little noise, moving quickly along the passageways. As they continued onward, the children felt the air grow warmer and warmer. A short while later, the heat grew uncomfortable and they began to sweat.

After what seemed like hours of steady marching, they finally saw light up ahead. "At least we can see what's going on," thought Gwendolyn. "I suppose it makes little difference, however, with our feet and hands tied together."

The tunnel opened on to the ledge of a vast cavern that disappeared into the darkness above. But nearer to them, everything was illuminated by a reddish glow which came from below. The children looked down and gasped. A great lake of fire stretched out below them. It hissed and bubbled, belching up great clouds of steam. The trolls slowed, and were careful to stay as far back from it as possible, clearly uncomfortable so close to the hateful fire.

A thick, raised platform made of ancient stone ran around the rim of the lake, allowing one to walk along its edge to reach another tunnel entrance on the opposite side. In addition, a narrow stone bridge had been built directly over the lake, allowing one to stand above the lava-filled basin, though for what purpose, Gwendolyn couldn't tell. At the far edge of the cavern, she could see that large iron support beams strengthened the stone bridge on either side. She suspected that this must be the giant's old forge—Ozzo's Furnace—that Polonius had told them about earlier. Her suspicions were confirmed when she saw abandoned bellows, anvils, and metal-working tools scattered about the area where they were now standing.

The trolls dropped Gwendolyn and Aethelred onto the hard stone floor. Now that the children's eyes had adjusted once again to the light, they saw that there were four of them, each uglier than the next. A short distance away, with his back to the children, stood Gimlash, carrying the seed. Then Gwendolyn noticed something else. A small figure was standing in front of the troll leader, his face obscured by the creature's hulking frame. Gimlash bowed low, setting the seed on the floor at the person's feet before backing away slowly.

"Where is the third?" the figure asked. The voice was cold and hard, but also strangely familiar.

"We never found him, my lord," said Gimlash, sounding uncomfortable. "However, we caught these two in the tunnels to the east, just as you had predicted."

"No matter," replied the voice. "You have brought me what I need."

Gwendolyn exhaled. At least Polonius wasn't caught as she had feared. Where was he? Then a head peered out from behind Gimlash and she could see the figure to whom the troll spoke. She recognized the face immediately. So did her brother.

Gwendolyn's eyes widened. "Ghael?"

She looked at the Merovian boy as he walked towards them. He didn't appear injured. Instead, he stared back at her, examining her carefully. Had he been captured, too? Why wasn't he bound?

"Are you okay?" she gasped.

Ghael frowned at her and smirked slightly. The trolls laughed. Gwendolyn swiftly realized that Ghael was not their prisoner. He wore a sword, but it was much too big for him. He stood confidently in front of the creatures, with no trace of fear in his eyes.

"I am quite well, thank you," he replied. The trolls laughed louder while Ghael permitted himself a smile.

Gwendolyn was dumbfounded. "You're—you're with *them*?"

"Not quite," said the boy, smiling more broadly. "They're with *me*."

***

"You traitor!" yelled Aethelred.

"Mind your manners, boy!" Bogg snarled, kicking him viciously in the back. Aethelred writhed in pain, whimpering softly.

"Leave him alone," cried Gwendolyn, "or I'll take your other eye!" She strained against the ropes that bound her hands and legs, trying to summon the magic within her. However, nothing happened. The bonds held fast. Bogg approached her, raising his scimitar. Before he could reach her, Ghael put up his hand and the troll stopped.

"Traitor?" inquired Ghael, raising his eyebrows, and looking at Aethelred. "I have many names but that is not one of them."

"But you told Uncle Wulfric about Sköll's navy!" Aethelred replied, still confused. "Why would you warn him of the attack if you weren't trying to help us?"

"I needed to reach Valmar quickly and without incident," explained Ghael, haughtily. "What better way than by being escorted by your gullible uncle? As for my navy, it doesn't matter if your people have been warned. With the dragon having destroyed the castle, there is now nowhere for them to run."

"How could you do this?" cried Aethelred. "You're just a child. Like us!"

"Am I?" asked Ghael. "I suppose this charade is no longer necessary." The Merovian boy uttered a strange word. "*Transfiguro.*" All of a sudden he began to change. The children watched in horror as he grew taller and older before their eyes. A beard sprouted from his cheeks. His nose grew longer, and his eyes grew darker—and fiercer. His head soon resembled a vulture: bald, worn, and cruel.

In a moment, the transformation was complete. Ghael was now a fully grown man, and the sword he wore no longer dangled at his feet. The trolls knelt before him. Gwendolyn got the impression that they weren't as surprised by this change as she and Aethelred, but they were intimidated by the man's appearance nonetheless.

"As I said, I have many names," said the strange figure standing before them. "Tyrant. Vengeance. Death." He cackled. "My subjects, however, eventually learn to call me Lord Sköll."

The children were stunned. Was it possible? Gwendolyn had heard of some magicians powerful enough to change shape. She had, however, never imagined Sköll to be one of them. What else could he do? What would become of them now that Polonius was gone? The trolls would surely eat them if given Sköll's permission. She grew afraid as these questions crowded her mind.

Gwendolyn took a deep breath and closed her eyes. She remembered what the gryphon said about fear. It was fear that had hardened her father's heart, preventing him from asking the giants for help. Unless men learned to rule their fear, they would be ruled by it. With this in mind, she returned to her previous thoughts and approached them differently. Yes, Polonius was gone, but he had not been captured. He would certainly be looking for them. That comforted her. Then she thought of something else. Sköll wouldn't simply hand them over to the trolls until the children had served his purpose. He needed them. Otherwise, why were they still alive? Gwendolyn was determined to frustrate his plans as long as possible until Polonius returned. But first she had to know what he wanted.

"Why have you brought us here?" she demanded.

Sköll looked down at her contemptuously. "You're going to help me awaken the seed."

"We'll never help you!" cried Aethelred, still struggling against his bonds.

Sköll turned angrily towards the boy. "No?" he sneered. "Then perhaps I should just give you to the trolls?"

"Yes, give him to us!" they slobbered, coming forward, despite being wary of the fiery lake below.

Aethelred's face turned white with fear, which pleased Sköll. He wanted to frighten the boy even more.

Turning to the trolls he asked, "Do you know who these children are?"

"Valmarian pups!" replied one.

"Dinner!" barked another.

Sköll shook his head. "These are the direct descendants of Edubard the Terrible!" he said. "Surely you know that name?"

The trolls gnashed their teeth and howled. It was Edubard son of Childeric who had been responsible for killing so many of their kind in the wars long ago. The thought of Edubard's heirs in their midst enraged them.

Overcome with hatred, Bogg reached out to grab Gwendolyn. Quick as lighting, Sköll drew his sword and cut off the troll's great arm. He screamed and collapsed, clutching his bloody stump while the other three trolls backed away fearfully. After a moment, Bogg tried to stand, moaning and crying out for help. However, dizzy from the pain, he slipped in this own blood and fell again to the ground. He did not get up.

"Patience!" cried Sköll, holding up his sword. "The troll army will have its revenge on both the Valmarians and on the giants. Your attack can wait one more day. First, however, I need her power!"

Sköll wiped his blade on Bogg's body before sheathing the weapon. He looked at Gwendolyn, his eyes blazing with an unnatural light. "You must restore the full measure of magic to the dragon seed."

"I don't know what you're talking about," said Gwendolyn. "Even if I did, I don't know where it is!"

"Oh, I think you do," replied Sköll, smiling. "After all, you led these trolls right to it." Sköll enjoyed seeing the panic in the children's eyes. He laughed again as he walked back a few paces to pick up the seed that Gimlash had set at his feet. "It's fortunate that your brother is so good at guessing riddles," said Sköll. "Otherwise, we might still be digging under Ballan á Moor." Then he held up the seed.

Seeing it clearly for the first time, the children could only watch in silent wonder. As Sköll raised it above his head, it glowed brightly, filling the cavern with sharp, clear light. Normally, trolls could tolerate firelight though they preferred the dark. Now that the seed shone fiercely, they cursed and shielded their eyes, backing away further into the shadows.

Gwendolyn grew angry. She was finally face to face with the tyrant that she had dreamed of defeating. He had deceived her uncle and parents, playing upon their hopes of victory even as his navy prepared to attack Ballan á Moor. Now he was here to exploit the dragon seed's power. Gwendolyn could only imagine what he would be like if he could harness its energy. Perhaps worst of all, he conspired with trolls. No man who had ever lived, however wicked, had befriended these loathsome creatures before.

"If you have it, why do you need me?" she asked, controlling herself.

"Why indeed?" Sköll responded. "I have studied magic all of my life. I have learned to change my appearance, infect my enemies with fear, and communicate great distances with certain . . . allies." He looked at the trolls and smiled. "A dragon's egg is a rare prize indeed. However, you must first return what Childeric stole from it."

"I cannot give you what I do not have!" cried Gwendolyn. She still wasn't sure what he meant, but she knew he intended to use the seed in some way that would ultimately hurt it—just as he hurt everything else. She again felt protective towards the seed and was determined to thwart his will.

"Yes you will," he said, decisively. "You must lay your hands on it just as your great-grandfather did all those years ago."

"What good will that do?" she asked, baffled by his words.

"The magic in your veins will flow back to its source," he replied, "making the seed whole again."

12

METAMORPHOSIS

Sköll had been waiting years for this moment. Twelve years to be precise.

Shortly after conquering Valmar he had learned that the trolls, which men thought nearly extinct since the great wars, had steadily grown again in number in the Solitary Marshes. From there, the creatures had tunneled west into the foothills of the Skelding mountains where they continued to burrow under rock and tree, fen and glade, until one day they discovered the Low Road.

Finding it abandoned by both men and giants, the trolls were surprised and delighted to learn that it led directly from the western foothills of the mountains all the way to Ballan á Moor, the scene of their bitter defeat all those years ago. More importantly, they remembered that Childeric's legendary seed was believed to be buried under the castle. So they had begun searching for it earnestly among the catacombs, thinking that Childeric, in his cleverness, had built the maze to keep others from finding his prize.

It was during this time, when Sköll was in Valmar instructing Argus about what he must do to keep his family alive, that the trolls had sent a secret ambassador named Shadrock to visit the Merovian king. Shadrock congratulated Sköll on his victory, and made him an offer. If the trolls found the dragon seed, they would make a present of it to Sköll—for trolls did not know how to wield magic any more than they knew how to read. In return, Sköll must abandon the kingdom of Valmar, allowing the trolls to take their revenge upon men.

When he had learned that the trolls were already actively digging under Ballan á Moor, Sköll was first annoyed by their interference. Why didn't these monsters simply stay in the marshes where they belonged instead of bothering him with such fairy tales? The Valmarians would pay him good tribute while remaining under his control. When Shadrock told Sköll about the Low Road, however, and how it led from Ballan á Moor all the way to the mountains, another thought occurred to him. If true, the Low Road would allow the Merovians to reach the very doors of Grimstad unseen. With the help of the trolls, he could surprise the giants with his army before they had a chance to prepare for a siege! Let them close their great iron gates against him! Without enough time to gather food and water, they would soon be forced to fight—weakened and exhausted—or surrender. He knew that the giants, while strong, were few in number. Grimstad could be his! Then, the trolls could have Argus and his family. That was but a small matter when compared to the chance of controlling the entire island.

As for the legend of the lost dragon seed, Sköll considered it nothing but a fable. He did not, however, tell that to Shadrock. Instead, he encouraged the trolls to continue looking for the seed. This, he thought, would focus their energy on digging instead of growing restless enough to fight the Valmarians prematurely. It also gave Sköll time to collect enough tribute from Argus and his people to pay for the army that would eventually march on Grimstad. Armies cost money—lots of money—and Merovia's coffers needed years to replenish. More importantly, Sköll had become alarmed by the rumors of poor morale among his men. Some of his officers had grown tired of war and had begun to openly grumble about being away from home for so long. So Sköll patiently waited for years while his reserves grew large enough to pay for the Merovians and mercenaries needed to invade Valmar once again.

Now, after all that time, he was ready. Sköll had gathered his fleet in Moska (as Wulfric had witnessed) and prepared to set sail. The plan was simple. He would once again invade the kingdom of Valmar, taking Ballan á Moor by surprise, before subduing Argus and his people. Then, guided by the trolls along the Low Road, Sköll's army would secretly reach the gates of Grimstad where they would surprise the giants.

As he was making final preparations in Moska, however, one of his most trusted spies, Perfidius, informed him of a strange ship docked in the harbor. Perfidius said that though it looked like an eastern trading ship from Quintharia, it fit the description of the pirate ship that had been harassing and plundering Sköll's trading ships for three years.

"Are you sure of this?" demanded Sköll.

"Yes, my lord," replied Perfidius. "We have been piecing together information on this vessel for years, and all of the descriptions fit. Just give the order, and we will storm the ship."

After reflecting on this development for a few moments, Sköll spoke. "No." He smiled as he saw the look of confusion spread across Perfidius's face. "I will deal with this myself."

"But my lord —"

Sköll narrowed his eyes. "Do you doubt me, Perfidius?"

"No, my lord," responded the other man, careful not to make eye contact with his king.

"Of course you don't—and you never should," said Sköll. "If what we suspect is true—if this ship is manned by Valmarians—then perhaps I have found a way into Valmar ahead of the fleet."

"How will you do that, my lord?" asked a confused Perfidius.

"Leave that to me," replied Sköll. "If I am not back by evening, assume that I have set sail on this ship to Valmar. The fleet is to follow as scheduled. With any luck, Ballan á Moor will be mine before you reach Valmar. Now go!"

As Perfidius hurried out of the room, Sköll smiled, pleased with himself. These pirates had evaded his navy for years by constantly assuming new disguises for their ship. Now, it was his turn to adopt a disguise. Raising his hands above his head, Sköll slowly chanted a few strange words, repeating them over and over. His chanting grew faster and faster, and soon he began to shrink. His beard disappeared, as did the deep lines under his eyes. In a moment, he looked like a young Merovian boy.

How ironic, he thought, that the same Valmarian ship that had caused his trading vessels so much grief would smuggle him into Valmar to destroy it. Now that his transformation was complete he conceived a plausible story to get on board. He would begin by telling them what they already suspected: the ships in Moska's harbor were indeed an invasion force. But how would he convince the ship's captain to take him to Valmar? Even easier. Tell him the invasion force was coming for Ballan á Moor and that he, Ghael, was Sköll's nephew who feared for his life. That should put some wind in the pirates' sails! When he landed at Ballan á Moor, he would simply sneak away to rally the troll army, invading the castle from beneath, and defeating the Valmarians before they knew what was happening.

However, even Sköll could not have anticipated Destiny's attack. Once he had fled with the rest of the Valmarians into the forest, horrible thoughts began to plague his mind. Even if he were able to lead the trolls to the surface to finish off the Valmarians, would anyone be safe with a dragon roaming the skies? And his approaching navy! It certainly wouldn't be safe from the giant lizard either. The dragon's presence threatened everything. Then, another thought occurred to him. What if the trolls were right? What if this lost seed was real, and the creature was searching for it?

That's when he had overheard Gwendolyn talking about the dragon in camp. The girl was somehow connected to the beast and seemed to have the dragon's power herself. That much he could understand—but he needed to know more. He kept an eye on her, eavesdropping on the children's conversation with Polonius later that evening.

When they had left camp, Sköll followed, remaining sufficiently behind them to avoid detection. He had lost them underground, however, when they fled eastwards toward Childeric's Keep, and had only met them unexpectedly when Polonius and Aethelred descended into the tunnel looking for Gwendolyn. There, the foolish boy had revealed to him that they believed they had discovered the seed's location. Could the legend really be true? Polonius's description of how Gwendolyn had used the dragon magic earlier that day seemed true enough. If so, the power of the seed could be Sköll's for the taking! He quickly retraced his steps, rousing four of the trolls. Then he sent them east to intercept the group and retrieve the seed while he formulated a plan. Now, at Ozzo's Furnace, he was ready for his greatest achievement yet.

The dragon seed was his—but not the dragon that lay inside of it. Not yet. For while Sköll possessed the egg physically, Gwendolyn still stood in his way. She was born with a magical power that rivaled his own though she did not know how to control it. There were other ways, however, to use the seed. He knew enough dragon lore to know that such seeds only give up their power once, when first touched by mortal hands. Had Edubard or the giants found the seed, they would not have been able to siphon more of its power.

Nor could the seed hatch until that power was restored to the dragon that lay inside the shell. But what if the shell could be penetrated by something *other* than dragon's fire? What if the creature could be forced to hatch? Could its will be bent to his bidding? Using his magic, he had broken the will of many creatures who now served him. Surely a dragon could be among them? And if he could control it, he could possibly defeat the other dragon—the one that threatened to undo all of his plans. The one they called Destiny.

Sköll held out the seed to Gwendolyn. "Call forth your magic and touch the seed," he demanded.

Gwendolyn glared at him. "No!"

"No?" asked Sköll, in a strangely calm voice. "I grow tired of asking." He turned to Gimlash. "Show the boy how dangerous the bridge can be."

Gimlash ordered one of the troll's to carry Aethelred to the center of the span which overlooked the fire below. She saw the terror in her brother's eyes, and realized too late what they intended to do.

"Throw him in!" commanded Sköll.

"Stop!" cried Gwendolyn. A powerful surge of magic ripped through her arms, disintegrating her bonds, as she focused on the troll who held her brother. Before he could even scream, the beast disappeared into a cloud of ash. Aethelred fell on the stone bridge with a thud, as his bonds evaporated.

Gwendolyn was stunned. Had she really done that? Why could she not call on this power as she pleased? The thrill of magic was still crackling in her fingertips when something dropped into her lap. It was the dragon seed. Sköll's face floated above her, smiling wickedly. "You've found the magic inside of you," she heard him gloat. "Now give it back."

Before she could respond her hands were drawn to the seed like magnets. Instantly she felt her energy flow into the object as her heart beat faster and faster. Then the heat in her arms and her chest were also drawn into the seed. Her magic, she realized, was leaving her, flowing back to its source, leaving her cold and tired. It hurt terribly, like her heart was being pulled out of her chest. After a few moments, she was drained, lacking even the energy to lift her head.

She tried to remove her hands but to her astonishment the seed still held them fast. What more could it want? Then she felt a presence in her mind. The dragon's personality had somehow entered her consciousness. She could hear the creature's thoughts!

"My name is Kindle," he said. "Who are you?"

She could feel his intelligence, his curiosity, and his deep desire to be born. This dragon lacked the fear and hatred for men that seemed to define his mother. Instead, he showed only wonder at the world he sensed beyond his shell. She wanted to protect him but she didn't know how.

"My name is Gwendolyn," she thought. "Too many people want to use you. I tried not to let that happen—but I've failed."

Then she grew even weaker and her vision began to fade. What was happening? She could still feel the tingling sensation in her fingers, but now it felt as if her life force was slowly ebbing from her body. Kindle didn't understand what he was doing to her. If he didn't release her soon, she would be dead. Concentrating intently, she thought "You must let me go! Please!"

Instantly, her hands were released and the seed rolled slowly from her lap.

"Impressive!" said Sköll, picking up the seed, which glowed an intense green. "I didn't expect you to live."

Meanwhile, Aethelred had crept back across the bridge towards Gwendolyn. He stood over his sister, ready to defend her, but to his surprise he noticed that Gimlash and the other troll remained fearfully back in the shadows. Sköll, however, did not seem to care about the children's movements as he walked towards the edge of the lake of fire. Then Gwendolyn felt her brother whispering something in her ear. "Polonius!" she heard him say. "Polonius!" Yes, she thought. Poor Polonius. He had never come. Perhaps he had realized what had happened and had gone to tell her parents.

Her thoughts were interrupted by Sköll's words. "By being the first to touch the seed, Childeric absorbed some of its magic," he explained, staring at her with contempt. "Now that the seed has recovered that power from your blood line, it will never give it up again."

"Then why do you need it?" Gwendolyn asked weakly, propping herself up one elbow. "Leave the dragon seed alone! It will not hatch for you!"

"Let me guess," snorted Sköll. "Only a dragon's fire is hot enough to perform the task?"

"Yes," she replied. "Nothing else can penetrate its shell. You can't hurt him."

Sköll dangled the seed over the edge of the precipice. "Let's put that to the test, shall we?" Then, he dropped it into the lake of fire.

"No!" shouted Gwendolyn, jumping to her feet.

The children ran to the edge and looked over. The seed floated on the lake's molten surface, engulfed in flames. However, it did not melt. Instead its glittering shell slowly turned black, dimming the cavern again.

Gwendolyn was horrified. "What have you done?" she said angrily, turning to Sköll. "Why have you destroyed him? He did nothing to you!"

He smiled back at her. "Behold," he replied, never taking his eyes from the seed. "The fire makes all things new!"

Aethelred pointed at the fire below. "Gwen, look!"

She turned and saw that the seed had changed. It was still black but it was growing larger. Much larger. Then she noticed cracks slowly spreading along its surface, revealing a green light underneath.

She heard one of the trolls bellow in pain. Gwendolyn and Aethelred turned to see Polonius exchanging blows with one of the two remaining trolls. Where had he come from? There was no time to ask questions for at that moment Gimlash caught Polonius across the chin with one of his giant fists, sending the old man sprawling. The second troll sprang forward, its scimitar drawn, and attacked Polonius where he lay. Just before the blow fell, however, Polonius jumped to his feet and lunged to the right. Then, he drew his battle axe and stepped backwards. The trolls closed ranks and walked toward him carefully, determined not to let him escape again.

They expected him to either continue backing away— or more likely—flee back down the tunnel behind him. Instead, he did the opposite, charging the beasts and swinging his axe with impressive aim.

The cavern rang with the sound of metal as Gimlash parried his blow. The other swung at Polonius but the old man ducked and ran on to the bridge. The trolls were in such a rage that they turned and gave chase, ignoring the fiery lake below. Polonius continued to retreat until he was in the center of the span. The bridge was only wide enough for one to pass. Her tutor had evened the odds by occupying it. The two trolls could now only attack him in single file.

The trolls realized this too. Gimlash continued to advance toward Polonius while the other ran along the outer edge of the ridge to approach him from the other side. Soon, they would be able to attack him from both directions of the bridge at once. It would be impossible for Polonius to win!

Then Gwendolyn understood her tutor's true purpose. By luring the beasts on to the bridge, Polonius had caused the trolls to leave the cavern's entrance unguarded. The children could escape! The thought of being free from this place was tempting. However, they refused to abandon Polonius.

Aethelred picked up the dead troll's scimitar in both hands and held it unsteadily. It was clearly too large for him. Nevertheless, he looked at his sister and pretended to be brave. "We must help him," he said.

"Put that down, boy!" said a cruel voice. They had forgotten Sköll! He had drawn his sword and was advancing towards them, his eyes black and cold.

"Don't you go near my brother," replied Gwendolyn, standing in front of Aethelred.

Sköll smiled. "You've served your purpose," he murmured, raising his sword. "I'll kill you both in one stroke."

Then they heard a roar that caused everyone's heart to quail in fear. Gwendolyn looked up and saw a creature emerge from the flames, his wings spread wide as he rose into the air. The dragon had hatched!

Though still small compared to a fully mature dragon, he was much larger than any troll (or even a giant for that matter). His green scales still smoked from the lake's heat but judging by the swiftness with which he moved he appeared unharmed. The dragon hovered directly over Gwendolyn, and she was struck by the beauty and intelligence of his eyes. Then she heard a voice inside of her head.

"So *you* are Gwendolyn," he said. "But who are the others?"

171

How he recognized her was a mystery. Before she could speak, however, she heard Sköll chanting in a hypnotic voice. It sounded like a spell. He sheathed his sword and held out his hands to the dragon, smiling.

Buried under scarp and stone,
Mountain peaks and bleached bones
In caverns deep where time's unknown,
You slept O seed of Destiny!

I have known your restless dreams
And came to quell your fearful screams.
Serve me now to be redeemed
And rise O seed of Destiny!

Rise and flee your ancient tomb
As you did your earthen womb!
Serve me now or face your doom
O mighty seed of Destiny!

The dragon continued to hover above Gwendolyn in the warm air, beating his great wings. He switched his gaze to Sköll as his eyes dilated. The Merovian king smiled wickedly, confident his enchantment was working. The dragon was under his power. It did not matter now that his plan to surprise Grimstad or Ballan á Moor had been delayed. Soon, nothing would stand in his way.

Then the dragon spoke. "You who claim to know me," he growled, staring down on Sköll, "what is my name?"

Sköll looked confused. His spells had never failed before. "Your name?" he asked, nervously. "You are Destiny's seed!"

"No!" growled the dragon. "My *name*."

Sköll grew more agitated and tried again. "You are Fire Blossom!" he cried. "Childeric's Bane! Air Crawler! Gold Seeker!" The dragon, however, simply shook his head at each wrong answer.

Gwendolyn stepped forward. "No," she said, softly. "His name is Kindle."

The strong connection that had been created between them somehow remained. The dragon acknowledged her words and bowed his head low.

Sköll was shocked. How did the girl know? He slowly began backing away towards the cavern's entrance but the dragon's tail quickly coiled around his legs, lifting him high in the air.

"You wished to use me for ill," said Kindle. "Perhaps when your spirit leaves your body as I have left my shell you will find peace, though you do not deserve it!"

Then Kindle flung Sköll over the edge, where he fell shrieking to his doom into the lake of fire. Finally, the man who had plagued Gwendolyn's family for more than a decade was no more.

She looked up and saw Polonius alone on the bridge. A dead troll lay sprawled at his feet. But where was Gimlash? Seeing Gwendolyn's bewilderment, her tutor shouted, "The other troll has fled! We must leave this place before they return in force!"

She turned to Kindle. "Polonius, Aethelred, and I may still be able to escape using the tunnels," she said, anxiously. "Even you, however, cannot resist an army of trolls when trapped underground! What will you do?"

The dragon looked up into the darkness above. "If I cannot find a way out, I will make one."

13

DANGEROUS WATERS

Soon after Gwendolyn, Aethelred, Polonius, and Ghael had disappeared, the king and queen had ordered a massive search of the forest. Argus and Thelda guessed that they had secretly left camp to ask the giants for help, ignoring the king's earlier command. Argus, Wulfric, and others searched miles of the forest in vain, and even risked returning to Ballan á Moor to examine the ruins under open sky. As night fell, however, they found nothing.

When the search failed, Thelda thought her husband would be angry. She braced for his explosive reaction. Instead, Argus shrugged, and quietly went back to his work preparing for the Merovian invasion. The queen knew that this response was worse than any outburst. It was the behavior of a man who had despaired—and now only pretended to govern as king.

Wulfric understood this as well. Though he would never dream of deposing his brother, he also knew that unless he took drastic action, Valmar would surely be lost. Something had to be done—and soon.

Having seen the Merovian navy up close, Wulfric knew it consisted of at least forty ships, each outfitted with a crew of four dozen fighting men, and sixteen heavy cannons. As a result, these ships sat low in the water, and maneuvered slowly. He also knew that he and his crew could easily out sail them. However, they were the only fighting ship that Valmar had, since they had been forbidden by Sköll to maintain a navy. Besides, Wulfric understood that this was not a question of naval tactics. The Merovians would not chase his ship. They were intent upon landing at Ballan á Moor and subduing its people. With the castle almost destroyed, the Merovians' job would be that much easier. There was nothing to stop them when they landed.

Nevertheless, Wulfric urged his brother to fight Sköll's navy when it arrived, attacking the invading army on the beach. "Better to die on our feet, than to be hunted in the forest like foxes, brother!" argued Wulfric, passionately.

"If most of our people were trained fighters like us, I would agree," replied Argus gravely. "But most are not soldiers. They have never wielded a sword or a bow in their lives. It would not be a battle, Wulfric. It would be a slaughter."

Wulfric knew his brother was right. However, he didn't think the king's plan was any better. "Hiding in the forest is not a strategy!" he said, trying to keep his anger in check.

"Unless you can convince the fish to fight Sköll's navy for us," declared Argus, "it is the only choice we have."

Wulfric pulled at his lip. Suddenly, his eyes widened— and then narrowed. "I need sheep."

***

When Wulfric and his crew had fled Valmar three years earlier, they had sailed north, hoping to avoid the Merovian warships that patrolled the seas. The fishing boat they had taken, while fast enough to escape Sköll's navy on the open ocean, lacked the cannons and other weapons they would need to defend themselves if surrounded. Wulfric knew that if they met the enemy unprepared, they would be hopelessly outmatched.

There was another reason, however, for venturing into the North Sea. The Moaning Isles, a group of six small islands clustered together in the chilly waters there, was home to a people that shared Valmar's fate. It, too, was conquered by Sköll's navy shortly after Wulfric's country was subdued. The people were also held hostage by Sköll's ridiculous laws, which included that they fish only within sight of shore. Predictably, they hated him. However, with no army or navy to defend their home, they continued to pay tribute to Merovia's oppressive king. Wulfric hoped that the people of the Moaning Isles would look upon him as an old friend and perhaps help him disguise his ship so that he would not be recognized when plundering Merovia's trading vessels in the future.

One evening, as Wulfric sailed into Brae, the capital of the Moaning Isles, the people greeted him and his men kindly—but also with surprise. The only foreign vessels they had seen in years had been Merovian merchant ships escorted by larger warships. The governor of the Moaning Isles, a bald, fat man named Lord Dravius, had received them with warmth and generosity, even lending them his shipbuilders to camouflage their vessel's true origin. He had known both Wulfric and Argus for many years before the Merovians prevented the two island nations from trading with one another. Dravius disliked paying tribute to Sköll as much as anyone. Like Valmar, however, he could do nothing against Merovia's might.

As Wulfric and his men prepared to leave, they thanked Dravius and his people for their hospitality. "It is our pleasure, Wulfric," said Dravius, a proud man like Argus. "You have already proven your bravery."

"Thank you, old friend," replied Wulfric. "One day, we will throw off the heavy chains of Sköll's tyranny. However, I have proven nothing so far—except, perhaps, that I needed your help."

"On the contrary," protested the bald man. "Our people said they saw your ship coming directly from the waters to the south. You have shown great courage by daring to sail past the serpent. Merovia's navy is a mere trifle compared to that creature."

Wulfric frowned. "The serpent?"

"Yes," said the governor of the Moaning Isles. "The beast that has haunted the deep waters of the North Sea for several years now." The old man studied Wulfric's face. "It is as blue as the sea—save for its eyes. Those are as red as embers." He paused. "You mean you did not know?"

"I'm afraid not," admitted Wulfric, chagrined. "You speak of a sea monster?"

"The largest I've ever seen," declared Dravius, marveling at Wulfric's luck. "We call it the serpent, for it resembles a giant snake—but I assure you it can do things that no snake can."

Wulfric was intrigued. "How so?"

"It is scaly like a serpent, you see, but it can also extend those scales until they become barbs," replied Dravius. "There are tales of it swimming up alongside a ship and ripping the wooden hull apart in seconds. When it catches those unfortunate sailors in the water, it doesn't have to wait long."

"Wait for what?" As soon as Wulfric asked the question, he realized the answer.

"To feed," responded Dravius, shuddering at the thought.

"Merovian ships still come and go from here," he objected. "How do they avoid such a beast?"

"They are careful to come and go from the west," explained Dravius. "The serpent is territorial, remaining south of the Moaning Isles—always south. Why, I do not know. Since you and your men traveled right through its hunting grounds, you should consider yourself fortunate to still be alive."

"What about your fishing boats?" asked Wulfric. "Are they not afraid of this beast?"

Dravius shook his head. "The serpent has never attacked a ship that remains close to the isles," he said. "For reasons still unknown to us, the creature prefers the deep water."

Wulfric thanked Dravius again before setting sail with his crew. This time they were careful to leave from the west. They would rather encounter a dozen Merovian warships than risk the serpent's domain.

***

Normally, Argus would have asked his brother why he needed sheep. The king, however, now barely spoke. "Take what you need," he said, not seeming to care. "By morning, they'll be dead anyway."

Wulfric knew he didn't have a moment to lose. Early the next morning, he gathered his men in the forest and they returned to the ship with as many sheep as they could find. Then the sails were unfurled and the sea breeze blew them slowly out into deeper waters. Wulfric addressed his men from the quarter deck. "My brothers!" he cried. "You who have fought and bled with me these three years—are you ready for our greatest adventure yet?"

"Yes, captain!" they shouted. "Show us the way!" The crew loved Wulfric, for he had proven his bravery time and time again by personally leading the raiding parties during their pirate days. More important, when he had convinced them to leave the kingdom of Valmar, and make new lives at sea, he had given them back the most essential part of themselves—their freedom. Now they would never again endure the injustice of Sköll's rule. His men also knew, however, that they were one ship, and miserably outnumbered by Sköll's fleet. Nevertheless, they were sailors who, if they had to die, preferred to die fighting.

"Then we sail north!" cried Wulfric.

The sailors looked at each other, bewildered. North? But Sköll's army was attacking from the south. Were they fleeing from the enemy? Wulfric understood their confusion, and he smiled back at them.

"We will fight," he promised, grinning impishly. "First, however, we're going fishing."

***

Kindle leaped into the air and disappeared into the darkness above. Gwendolyn, Aethelred, and Polonius stared at one another, bewildered. Where had he gone? Then they heard a great explosion. Sunlight streamed down on them, illuminating the cavern—followed by giant chunks of falling rock. Kindle had broken through the top of the volcano!

"Quick!" shouted Polonius. "Back to the cavern's entrance!" The three barely had time to take shelter in the tunnel as the remnants of the caldera crashed down into the center of the lake, causing molten rock to spill over the banks. The fallen stones shattered the center of the bridge and it collapsed into the flames below.

In the tunnel behind them they heard the sound of rushing feet and deep voices. The troll that had fled after Sköll's death had returned with reinforcements. Now that Gwendolyn and Aethelred had seen and heard trolls, the sound of their harsh cries was unmistakable.

"We cannot go this way!" declared Polonius. "We must try the opening on the other end of the cavern!" They re-entered the forge but quickly discovered this way was now dangerous as well. Most of the large rocks above them had already fallen. However, fist-sized stones continued to rain down around them. Making matters worse, hissing pools of lava slowly spread into the path that circled the lake.

Following Polonius, the children picked their way across the edge of the cavern, avoiding the hissing puddles of molten rock. They were grateful for the sunlight, which helped them to see clearly, but they still had to watch for falling stones. They had not gone far, however, when they heard the wild shouts of trolls coming from the cavern's entrance behind them. "Faster!" urged Polonius.

They ran as fast as they could—but it was no use. Despite the sunlight, the trolls moved swiftly, especially now that they were angry. In a moment, the creatures were at the children's heels, slobbering and snarling as they came. Realizing that they could not outrun their enemies, Polonius stopped and turned to fight. He raised his battle axe above his head as Gwendolyn and Aethelred ran past him. It would be over very soon now, he thought. He would gladly die if he could give the children time to escape.

Suddenly, a great shadow descended upon the foremost troll. A second later, a fireball consumed the wretched creature. Polonius lowered his weapon and looked up, astonished.

Kindle had returned.

The dragon's landing shook the ground as the trolls stumbled and then stopped, amazed and terrified by his appearance.

Kindle looked at Polonius and the children. "On my back!" he commanded. Desperate to escape, they scrambled up the beast's enormous shoulders. Kindle's scales were smooth and hard like shields, but with deep crevices, allowing them to curl their fingers around the edges.

Kindle leaped into the air. "Hold on!" he said. Gwendolyn watched as her attackers fell away below, cursing and gnashing their teeth as they shook their scimitars. They continued to fill the cavern like angry ants but they could only shout in rage as their prey escaped. Gwendolyn couldn't believe their number. There must have been hundreds. How many more trolls hid in the tunnels under this mountain?

Her thoughts changed as Kindle cleared the icy, uneven rim of the volcano. Gwendolyn had been underground for so many hours that the sight of the sun shining in the bright blue sky startled her. Her face grew numb in the cold mountain air and she had to narrow her eyes to look forward as her long black hair streamed behind her. Then she looked down. The Skelding mountains stretched away in all directions, revealing deep valleys of alpine forests. Far to the west, beyond the snowy peaks, lay the sea.

Looking over at her fellow passengers, Gwendolyn suppressed a smile. Aethelred had closed his eyes and was hanging on to the dragon like a cat in danger of falling into cold bath water. Polonius for his part was wide-eyed with fright. Her tutor didn't like heights but he was even more afraid of the dragon himself. Only Gwendolyn seemed to be enjoying the ride.

She heard Kindle's voice inside of her head. "Where shall we go?" he asked.

Gwendolyn thought of Ballan á Moor. She wanted to see her parents again. More importantly, her people could use a dragon's help. Kindle, however, had already saved her life twice. Why should he risk his life in a fight that was not his? It was unfair to assume he would help her again. She thought of the army of trolls they had just seen. The creatures would hide no longer. Soon, Gwendolyn knew, the mountains would be swarming with them. Then Gwendolyn remembered that Polonius had said Grimstad, the giant stronghold, was near. But where?

"Polonius!" she shouted. It was difficult to hear over the rush of wind in their ears, but she caught his eye. Her tutor leaned closer to her, still clutching the dragon's scales tightly. "Where is Grimstad?" she shouted.

Scanning the mountain range below, Polonius motioned with his chin. "There!"

Following his gaze, she at first saw nothing. Then, looking more closely she identified a small structure on the side of one of the mountains far below. She called upon Kindle in her mind. "There is a castle almost directly below us," she thought. "Take us there." Dragons have much better eyesight than most creatures, and Kindle quickly saw the castle and descended.

As they drew nearer, Gwendolyn realized Grimstad only seemed small from such a great height. In fact, the castle was enormous, straight, and proud, like the giants themselves. The structure gleamed white in the sunshine, and its walls were shaped like a pentagon. Each corner was anchored by a mammoth tower which looked down imposingly on the valleys below. Beyond the walls of the fortress, the giants had cut five great steps or plateaus into the mountainside, each supported by large retaining walls. Flocks of sheep and goats, which the giants used for milk and wool, grazed peacefully on these grassy fields as the dragon approached.

Kindle landed on the uppermost plateau at the base of the castle, scattering the frightened animals in all directions. Gwendolyn looked up at Grimstad's ramparts, and saw giant sentries running to the towers, shouting in alarm. The next moment, a bell tolled frantically from inside the castle.

"Well, at least they know we're here," she said, sliding easily from Kindle's back. Polonius and Aethelred quickly followed. They were thankful to be on solid ground once more. Gwendolyn, however, was a bit disappointed they could not have stayed airborne longer.

The dragon looked around curiously. "What is this place?"

"This is Grimstad, home of the Western Giants," explained Polonius, unable to believe he was speaking to a dragon. He still hoped Gwendolyn could make peace with the giants, but even he wasn't sure how they would be received with Kindle in their presence.

"Are they friend or foe?" asked the dragon, staring up at the white, granite walls.

"We're about to find out," replied Gwendolyn, watching the castle's huge portcullis open. Soon, three giants in bright red cloaks emerged and walked toward them. They were dressed in helmets and silver chain mail. Each carried long iron spears and large shields that spanned the length of their bodies.

Gwendolyn couldn't help but marvel at the solemn creatures as they approached. They were taller than trolls by several feet—and just as broad. They also showed neither fear nor hesitation, which must be difficult she thought, with a dragon on their doorstep. Stopping a few yards away, they pointed their spears at Gwendolyn and her friends. Then, one stepped forward and removed his helmet. His face was wrinkled with age, but his green eyes burned with a smoldering fire.

"Who are you—and why do you bring a dragon to our gates?" he demanded, gruffly, his breath visible in the cold mountain air.

The children's tutor stepped forward and bowed. "I am Polonius, a steward of Valmar and counselor to King Argus." He motioned towards the children. "Allow me to present Princess Gwendolyn and her brother, Prince Aethelred." The children bowed their heads. Then Polonius looked back at the dragon uncertainly, waving his arm. "This . . . is Kindle." The dragon simply stared back at the giants, making no movement.

The leader of the three giants looked unimpressed. "Why have you come?"

"We would discuss that directly with your king," said Polonius.

"He stands before you," declared the giant. "I am Ollom, son of Odom, grandson of Ozzo—and I am not frightened by you or any other scaled demons you've befriended." Kindle growled, causing the giants behind Ollom to shift uneasily. They stood their ground, however, with spears still pointed outward.

"We are not trying to frighten you," replied Gwendolyn, coming forward. "We've come to warn you that Grimstad is in grave danger." She quickly described her conversation with the griffon as well as the Merovian invasion, Sköll's death, and the army of trolls that seethed under their feet.

If Ollom was surprised at Gwendolyn's news, he certainly didn't reveal it. Instead, he narrowed his eyes. "Why do you tell us this?"

"The feud between us has lasted too long," she replied. "Besides, we cannot defeat both the Merovians and the trolls independently. We must work together—or we will die alone."

The king of the giants continued to stare down at them, stone-faced. Finally, he spoke. "You speak well, Gwendolyn of Valmar—for a human," he said. "However, I have dealt with well-spoken Valmarians before only to suffer betrayal. Many years ago, we helped Childeric defeat the trolls. In return, he promised us the dragon seed. But his son, Edubard, ignored his father's wishes and repaid us with evil, using a strange ancestral magic to kill many of my kin." He shook his head at the memory. "No, we know enough about men not to trust them. We will survive as we have always done—by remaining behind our walls."

"You also speak well, great king," said Polonius. "It is true that the giants have suffered at the hands of men." Ollom nodded his head in agreement. "These children are indeed too young to have witnessed the wars of which you speak. However, is it not also true that Childeric once saved your life?"

The giant king's face flushed red with anger. "That was long ago—when men were worthy of our trust. Now, however, men like yourself have become impertinent and foolish enough to think I need to be reminded of such things."

Polonius simply smiled. "You are three-quarters right."

"What do you mean?"

The old man folded his hands together and grinned, showing his sharp teeth. "I am also part giant—a descendent of Ozzo himself."

The two warriors behind Ollom murmured to one another while the giant king's eyes widened in surprise. Finally, he nodded. "I see in your features that you speak truly—but that does not answer for Edubard's betrayal of his father's promise to us. Until that debt is paid, there can be no peace."

Gwendolyn sighed in frustration. "What would you do if you were given this seed?"

"We would learn to use its magic just as men have done," replied the giant, passionately. "We would no longer live in fear of the power that flows in your veins."

It was as she suspected. The giants were also afraid of men! Why did fear seem to govern the world? Why did power cause so much distrust? "Then fear no more!" she cried. "For the magic that I once possessed has returned to its source."

"But the magic that Childeric promised us," demanded Ollom. "Where is it?"

"It was never his to promise," she said, her eyes sparkling as she looked up at Kindle. "Now it can never be exploited again—now it is whole."

Ollom looked at her confused. Then his eyes widened as he understood. "The seed that was lost has been found," he whispered, looking at the dragon as if for the first time. "The curse has been lifted!"

"Yes," said Kindle sternly. "The magic that you once thought a treasure has become a curse, causing you to live in fear of one another." He shook his head in frustration. "Neither of your races is as noble as you may think, though I do not know what lies in your souls." He turned to Gwendolyn and his expression softened. "However, thanks to the magic we once shared, I know this girl had the courage to protect me while I was still a seedling." Gwendolyn smiled.

As he watched them, Ollom's earlier bravado gave way to doubt. He knew that the trolls had indeed grown in number and had tunneled deeply under the earth. He remained confident, however, that he and his fellow giants could resist any attack. Then Gwendolyn and her friends had arrived, speaking of an army of trolls who would soon be swarming Grimstad. The giants were strong but had they underestimated the trolls? He thought of the Merovians. They had already conquered the Valmarians once. Why would they invade the island again if they did not mean to occupy it for good? Perhaps the girl was right. Perhaps peace between giants and men was the only way forward.

Despite the dragon's words, however, the thought of Edubard's betrayal still galled Ollom. How could he be sure of Gwendolyn's sincerity? There was one way to find out. "Very well," he declared. "We will agree to help Valmar fight the Merovians."

Gwendolyn's heart leaped with joy.

"On one condition," he added. "If the trolls are coming to attack Grimstad, you and your friends must help to defend our city first, as any good ally would." Ollom looked at Kindle as he spoke. The dragon would certainly be useful in a fight. "Perhaps in that way the promise made by your great-grandfather can still be honored."

Gwendolyn was torn. She desperately wanted to make peace between her people and the giants. She, however, was needed in Valmar. Kindle could sink Sköll's navy before it had the chance to land. Was it fair to ask Kindle to fight at all? The dragon knew her thoughts but he too was waiting for her answer—waiting to see her heart.

Finally, she spoke. "It will be as you wish!" she replied, decisively. "Let men and giants unite once again!"

Following his sister's lead, Aethelred bowed low. "Our people stand together!" he cried. Polonius also bowed in agreement. Gwendolyn, however, was not yet finished. She looked up at the dragon once more.

"Our swords are at your service but we cannot speak for Kindle," she said. "He is free, and shall remain so regardless of his decision."

They all looked at the dragon. Would he join them in a fight that was not his own? Or would he fly away to a distant land—and away from the coming war? Then he spoke. "I would be honored to fight alongside you and your allies, Gwendolyn of Valmar, wherever your courage leads you."

"Good!" Ollom grinned. "Then our friendship is now restored." He looked at the sun directly overhead. "There is much to do—and little time in which to do it. I just hope we survive the night."

14

THE SIEGE OF GRIMSTAD

In preparation for the coming siege, everyone capable of fighting girded for battle. The giants were a proud race and fierce warriors. However, they were few—no more than three hundred according to Gwendolyn's estimation as she entered the castle. Those too old or too young to fight huddled in a keep that stood in the center of the castle.

Polonius tried to convince the children to avoid the battle by staying well behind the castle's walls. He had hoped they could make peace with the giants but he had never planned on them fighting trolls so soon. Unfortunately, there was no stopping the children. Both had had some training in swordsmanship and insisted that they be allowed to help defend the castle. Impressed by their courage, Ollom honored the children by having armor made to suit them.

Giants were thoughtful gift givers and excellent craftsmen. We must forgive the blacksmith his smile, however, when he looked upon the leather jerkins and plate mail that he had hastily wrought for them. They seemed to him doll clothes. Nevertheless, they fit the children very well. Having lost their weapons in Ozzo's

Furnace, Gwendolyn and Aethelred were also given daggers from Grimstad's arsenal to use as two-handed swords.

As the sun fell behind the mountains, Polonius and the children stood with Ollom on the castle's ramparts waiting for the troll invasion. On top of each roofless tower along the castle's walls, the giants had placed great basins of oil which they had set on fire to help the sentries see the advancing enemy. Kindle sat in the courtyard, swishing his tail mischievously as he eyed a flock of sheep being herded past him.

Polonius put a hand on each of the children's shoulders as he looked into the valley below. "If the trolls breach the walls, stay near the fire beacons," he warned. "They will avoid the flames."

Ollom bristled. "I helped build Grimstad myself," he replied. "The trolls may try to climb our walls—but they will crash like seawater upon the rocks."

"I have no doubt," said Polonius, staring up at the moon. "However, there are other ways inside castles, as we have seen." Gwendolyn was about to ask him what he meant, when a great horn sounded. The troll army approached.

For years, the trolls had secretly burrowed under the mountains, closer to Grimstad. But the giant scouts had only guessed at their numbers in the last few months. They did not imagine that the creatures had once again grown so numerous. Now, the trolls filled the mountain passes near the castle, streaming out of hidden holes and cracks that they had previously disguised. Led by the sound of drums, their relentless approach sounded like thunder and their voices struck fear into the heart of even the bravest giant.

As they drew near, Gwendolyn could understand their words.

Shatter, clatter, splinter, break
We come to make your fortress shake!
Stomp, crush, smother, maim
We come to avenge our spoiled name!
Smash, gnash, slash, crash
We come to turn Grimstad to ash!

Then Gwendolyn saw them climb the plateaus in front of the castle and approach the main gate. There must have been a thousand or more. Unlike men or giants, the trolls did not march in an organized fashion. Instead, they swarmed toward Grimstad's high walls with astonishing speed. Some were trampled to death in their haste but their screams were drowned by the countless others who stepped over the twisted bodies.

The giant archers, who stood ready upon the battlements and towers, rained arrows down upon the attacking horde as it drew near. Many trolls were killed— but not enough. Soon, the archers had exhausted their arrows and looked helplessly down upon the sea of creatures below. The trolls produced great ladders which they used to scale Grimstad's granite walls. The guards on the battlements pushed these ladders backwards, sending the trolls crashing back to earth. For every ladder they repelled, however, two more would emerge from below. Soon, the trolls had gained the ramparts, fighting with a fury that amazed the giants.

The giants, however, still had hope. Most of the trolls did not know there was a dragon hiding behind Grimstad's high walls. It was almost time for Kindle to reveal himself. He had waited patiently until many of the creatures had emerged from the safety of the tunnels and were now gathered at the base of the castle, pounding the gates with their great warhammers. Now Kindle rose over the ramparts with deadly speed, swooping down upon the mass of trolls at the base of the castle as he rained down fire and death from above. In the confusion and terror, some of the trolls who had not been consumed by Kindle's flames slew one another in their panic. The giants cheered as they watched the trolls retreat downhill and back into the forest below. Ollom and most of the other giants decided to seize the advantage by opening Grimstad's iron gates before pursuing the enemy into the darkness.

After dispatching two trolls that had reached the ramparts, Gwendolyn and Aethelred stood alone near the north tower when they heard the sound of giants cheering below the wall.

Before they could peer over the battlements, however, a shadow fell upon them. A figure crept out of the darkness, holding a scimitar. As it drew near, the great cauldron of fire that burned on the tower illuminated the creature's cruel face. It was Gimlash! The troll recognized the children as well. His yellow eyes widened in surprise before narrowing again. "The heirs of Edubard the Terrible," he whispered. "I'm going to enjoy this."

The troll attacked Aethelred first, raising his scimitar over his head with both hands before bringing it crashing down upon him. The boy deflected the blow but the troll's strength was too great. Gimlash knocked the sword from Aethelred's grip and sent him sprawling backwards. The next moment, the beast stood over him, and thrust his sword toward the boy's chest. Before the blade reached him, however, Gwendolyn sprang forward and knocked it away with her weapon. Then, she surprised Gimlash, slashing wildly at the troll's legs. Her blade grazed his thigh and Gimlash stumbled backwards, which allowed Aethelred time to regain his footing. The troll roared in pain as they both turned and ran through the stone tower.

Gimlash gained on them quickly, however, howling like a crazed animal. Gwendolyn turned and brought up her blade just in time to stop the scimitar aimed at her back. She blocked another blow but she could no longer see her brother. Where had he gone? There was no time to think as she dodged the scimitar a third time. As the troll drove her backwards, raining more blows down upon her, she fell over a slain body lying near the edge of the battlements. She was momentarily defenseless.

But a moment was all the troll would need. Gimlash smiled and raised his scimitar above his head as he stepped toward her. She tried to bring up her sword again but realized she would be too late. To her surprise, though, the troll suddenly cried out and shot past her before plunging over the ramparts to his death. She looked up and saw Aethelred standing there grinning where the troll had been.

"What happened?" she asked, still breathing hard from the fight.

"When we passed the tower's doorway, I ducked behind the wall as he ran past," he explained, helping Gwendolyn to her feet. "Then, I followed you both. When Gimlash attacked you, I gave him a good push."

She hugged her brother closely. "That's the second time you've saved my life," she said.

They walked to the other side of the battlements and watched as the giants continued to chase the trolls away from the front gate into the darkness beyond. They looked at each other and smiled. Had the battle been won? Could it really be over?

They heard a cry in the courtyard below. It was Polonius. He and four other giants had been fighting a group of trolls that had made it down the ramparts. The creatures had been killed, but now Polonius and the giants were looking at the ground on which they stood and began to back away slowly. A rumbling could be heard coming from beneath the earth as a portion of the cobblestones began to shake. Then the stone collapsed altogether. Before the children understood what was happening, green hands and heads emerged from the ground. The trolls must have been tunneling under the castle even as the rest of their army attacked the outer walls.

As the creatures streamed out of the hole and attacked Polonius and others, Gwendolyn realized in horror that Ollom and many of his bravest warriors had left the castle to pursue the enemy into the forest. The trolls in the courtyard seemed to understand this too. They rushed to Grimstad's portcullis, shutting the iron doors firmly, preventing the giants from returning. This also meant that Polonius and the children were now locked inside, along with the rest of the giants. Gwendolyn and Aethelred looked back over the outer wall for some sign of Ollom's return. Instead, they saw only the pale moon watching them with indifference. Where were the giants? Where was Kindle?

More and more trolls continued to swarm out of the hole in the courtyard, attacking the small group of giants that had remained. Though they fought valiantly, the giants were quickly outnumbered, and they were forced to fall back, parrying one blow after the next. Then, out of the corner of her eye, Gwendolyn saw Polonius rushing toward the trolls, raising his battle axe. Was he mad? There were too many of them! A large troll strode forward, holding a warhammer. He swung at Polonius's head and just missed as the old man rolled forward, plunging his axe into the troll's leg. The beast squealed in pain and fell backwards. Soon, others rushed toward Polonius, surrounding him. He swung his axe in a circle keeping them at bay. But he was not fast enough. One of his attackers kicked him hard in the back and he fell forwards as his axe flew from his hands. The trolls loomed over him.

Thinking quickly, Gwendolyn rushed back into the tower, followed by her brother. There it was! The tower's fire beacon blazed fiercely in an enormous pool of oil. "Help me!" she shouted as she set her back against the flaming cauldron. Working together, the children pushed with all of their strength, upsetting the basin, which dumped flaming oil into the courtyard and on to the trolls below.

Polonius was still on his back when he saw the flames approaching. He rolled out of the way as the burning oil rained down upon them. Their howls could be heard for miles. Burning trolls ran wildly in circles, setting the others on fire. Gwendolyn remembered that trolls hated fire. The mere sight of it made them uneasy. Now with many of them engulfed in flames, chaos reigned below.

Aethelred tugged at her shoulder. "We must open the gates!" he cried. Of course! Gwendolyn tore her gaze from the grizzly scene and hurried with her brother to the battlements above the gate. There they found the large hand crank used to raise and lower the portcullis directly below. Drawing upon strength that they did not know they had, the children rotated the crank and slowly opened the gate. Many giants who had heard the sound of battle from beyond the walls now returned to finish the trolls.

The fight was over quickly after they had reached the courtyard. Many of the trolls had already burned to death or were so badly injured that they could not defend themselves. Gwendolyn and Aethelred turned away, not wanting to watch the slaughter. Instead, they looked over the walls again and saw Kindle returning from the forest with Ollom and the rest of the giants.

The troll army had been destroyed.

15

AN UNLIKELY ALLY

Hindered by a strong headwind, Wulfric and his crew had failed to reach the Northern Sea as quickly as they had hoped. It was now late in the morning and they were miles away from Valmar. They knew that Sköll's fleet would reach Ballan á Moor in just a few hours. Even if they were to reverse course now, there was no guarantee that they could return home in time to defend the island. To make matters worse, Wulfric's plan didn't seem to be working. Three sheep had already been killed and cast overboard—their white, bloated bodies could be seen trailing from behind the ship, attached to thick rope, untouched. The serpent was nowhere to be seen.

Using his spy glass, Wulfric watched the sheep bob up and down in the water about a hundred yards behind them. He heard the familiar footsteps of Melko approaching.

"What is it?" asked Wulfric, his eye never leaving the spy glass.

"Your plan is clever, captain," declared his first mate. He spoke in low tones so that no one else could hear him. "However, I'm afraid we're wasting our time."

Wulfric sighed. "What is the alternative, my friend?" he replied softly. "Shall we hope that the Merovians have forgotten the way to Valmar?" Still, he knew that if Melko was having doubts, the rest of the crew would be anxious, too.

"Forgive me, sir, but it would be better than returning to find our people already slaughtered."

Wulfric scoffed. "Against forty warships?"

"If necessary, yes." Melko folded his arms. "Perhaps we can lead them away from Ballan á Moor—lead them here?"

Wulfric shook his head and lowered the spy glass. He turned to his first mate. "Why would they chase us?" he asked. "What would they gain? No, Melko, the Merovians come for Ballan á Moor—and for the kingdom of Valmar. One ship means nothing to them. They would not give chase."

Suddenly, there was a shout from the crow's nest. They looked up and saw the sailor perched there yelling and pointing. Wulfric quickly raised his spy glass to his eye and saw only two sheep floating in the water. Where was the third? Then he gasped as an enormous white head rose from the waves. It swallowed one of the two remaining sheep in one bite before disappearing below.

He had only seen it for a moment but it was enough. The creature's eyes were as black as night and as wide as dinner plates. When it had opened its mouth, it had revealed two rows of teeth. Its milky scales glistened in the sun. Wulfric suspected that its body was thick as an oak tree and at least seventy yards long. They had found the serpent of the Moaning Isles.

"Bring her about!" he roared. "Full sail!"

Melko had also seen the monster. "To the oars!" he cried.

Instantly the deck sprang to life. Some sailors ran below deck, pulling hard at the oars to turn the ship around and increase its speed. Others scaled the riggings, unfurling every sail they could to harness the wind's power. Gratefully, Wulfric noted that while the stiff wind had hindered their course northward, it was now their ally, blowing them rapidly southward back towards Valmar. Then the serpent's great head reappeared for a moment, only to disappear again under the waves as it swallowed the third sheep.

Wulfric turned to Melko. "Throw a couple more overboard."

They had no time to kill the poor sheep as they had done with the others. The two animals bleated desperately as they were hastily thrown into the sea. A moment later, one disappeared. Then the other.

Wulfric rubbed his chin. "We should have brought more," he mumbled to himself, ruefully.

Though the sails were full and the men strained at the oars, he knew the ship had to go even faster if they were to reach Valmar in time—while also staying ahead of the sea serpent that trailed closely behind them. They continued to lure the creature south by tossing sheep overboard while Wulfric ordered some of his men to discard everything but the long boats tethered to the sides of the ship. Barrels of food and drink were thrown into the water, followed by heavy rope and extra bolts of sailcloth. Next, the crew's personal possessions were cast away. Finally, the ship's cannonballs and heavy cannons were abandoned to the deep.

Melko objected to Wulfric's last order. "Without our cannons, we will be defenseless," he pleaded.

"If we don't outrun the serpent, it won't matter!" replied the captain.

With these things gone, the ship was now very light and skipped quickly over the waves. Then the sailor in the crow's nest shouted again.

"I see it, sir! There, to the south! The Merovian fleet!"

Wulfric raised his spy glass to his eye once more. Dozens of masts and hundreds of red sails came into focus. Sköll's navy. He counted forty warships, about two leagues distant, sailing directly for Ballan á Moor's harbor. The ships sat low in the water, telling him that they carried many cannons on board as well as soldiers. If the Merovians saw Wulfric and his ship pursuing them, however, they took no measures to face them. He shook his head. They were probably not even looking behind them. Instead, they were intent only upon invading and ravaging the beautiful island that he called home.

"Put your back into it, men!" shouted Wulfric. "We must intercept them before they reach land!"

"But captain," said Melko, incredulous. "We have no cannons. They'll cut us to pieces if we get too close."

Wulfric glared at him for a moment. "I said *do* it."

They shot forward as the men doubled their efforts, grunting and straining at the oars below deck. Soon, they were within a league of the Merovian fleet—and closing fast. Wulfric no longer needed his spy glass. He could see the heavy cannons on the enemy ships clearly. He also saw hundreds of Merovians pointing at his vessel, apparently bemused by the recklessness of such an attack.

Wulfric saw white puffs of smoke appear on the rear of the ship nearest to them, followed a second later by the sound of cannon fire. "Get down!" he cried. Three cannon balls whistled dangerously overhead while everyone ducked. The shots, however, splashed harmlessly into the sea. Wulfric smiled in spite of the danger—or perhaps because of it. "Keep rowing!"

As he suspected, the Merovians didn't change course and face him. However, some of the ships slowed just enough to fire another volley, which also missed. Wulfric and his crew were now close enough to see the expressions of the Merovians themselves. They were grinning and even laughing at him and his crew. Sköll's orders were to land at Ballan á Moor and kill or capture every Valmarian that they could find. However, if a Valmarian ship had a death wish, they would happily oblige.

The Merovians fired again and this time they did not miss. The cannonballs tore through the ship's mast and sails, crippling the Valmarian vessel. The Merovian sailors laughed and shouted again, this time scolding Wulfric and his crew for their stupidity. Ignoring them, he shouted for the oarsmen to abandon the galley and return to the deck. The next moment, Wulfric felt the ship lurch and shudder—but it was not due to any cannonball.

"Lower the long boats!" he cried. "Abandon ship!" The Valmarians scrambled into the smaller boats and quickly lowered them into the sea as the ship filled with water.

The Merovian sailors cheered. The foolish Valmarians! Did they really think they could challenge such a mighty fleet? Instead, the madmen had been sunk without firing a single shot in return. They laughed and hooted as they prepared to aim their cannons at the long boats, picking off the cowards as they fled. Their laughter, however, turned to terror as a giant sea monster began to swim towards them.

"Row, men!" Wulfric yelled. "Row towards shore. Our lives depend on it!"

The Valmarians sprinted to the coast in the small boats, spurred on by the screams of the Merovians behind them. Wulfric allowed himself one last look. The close formation of the Merovian fleet allowed the serpent to work quickly, sliding along the wooden hulls with its white scales extended, ripping through them easily. The ships plummeted into the watery deep as the panic-stricken sailors jumped overboard, splashing helplessly in the tall waves. Wulfric watched in horror as some of the men continued to tread water, while others were pulled down below, one by one, never to be seen again.

The serpent would eat well today.

***

By the time the sun dawned on Grimstad the next morning, most of the troll bodies had been gathered in large piles and burned outside of the castle walls. Many brave giants had also lost their lives, however, and the mood was somber despite the victory. But Ollom knew it could have been much worse. Many more giants would have died if they had not been prepared for the attack. The sheep and goats they used to provide themselves with sustenance would have also been lost had they not been warned by Gwendolyn and her friends. And of course, Kindle's help had been invaluable during the battle.

Ollom was also told of the children's bravery and quick thinking on the ramparts, as well as Polonius's courage in the courtyard. Though some of the giants had initially distrusted the newcomers when they had entered the castle, they had proven themselves loyal friends. Even Kindle, whom the giants had once looked upon warily, was now regarded with smiles and nods. Soon, the giant children emerged from the interior of the castle, and made fast friends with the dragon. In the fields beyond the castle, they squealed in delight, taking turns sliding down his tail while Polonius and the children helped treat the wounded in the courtyard.

As she finished bandaging a giant's wounded hand, however, Gwendolyn's thoughts turned once again to Ballan á Moor. Had the Merovian navy already landed? Were her mother, father, and uncle still alive? How would her people resist another invasion with their castle destroyed? Then she saw Ollom approaching. After the battle, the king and his warriors had not slept. Instead, they had spent the night helping to bury the dead. She remembered that he had promised to help the Valmarians. However, that seemed like a lifetime ago. Would he and his people still have the strength or the desire to fight again so soon?

Ollom's mud-splattered face was lined with fatigue as he smiled down at her. "You took a great risk by coming here to warn us of the trolls, Gwendolyn," he said. "We will remember your bravery forever."

"There were many valiant deeds performed last night," she replied. "The victory belongs to your people."

"Indeed," he declared, wiping the mud from his face. "Many of my people died well last night. We will honor their memories. We will also honor our promise to you." Gwendolyn stood up and bowed low. Then Ollom spoke the words she had longed to hear. "I have ordered every one of my warriors who can still wield a weapon to be ready to march in one hour. We will fight for the Valmarians. We will fight to save your kingdom."

"Thank you," she replied, closing her eyes and smiling a little sadly. "I just hope there is still a kingdom left to save."

It was agreed that Gwendolyn, Aethelred, and Polonius would return to Ballan á Moor immediately on Kindle's back, while the giants would take the Low Road and approach from the south. Ollom explained that he and his soldiers would make good time by using boats on the underground river that ran parallel to the tunnel. "Look for us in the afternoon," he promised.

Polonius and the children climbed on Kindle's back before turning and waving to Ollom and the rest of the giants. "Farewell!" they cried.

"Farewell!" shouted the others in return. "We will come to fight for your freedom just as you have done for us!" Then Kindle beat his wings and rose into the air. In a moment they were barely visible, weaving in and out of the clouds as they streaked away north, back to Valmar.

***

Healing from her injuries high in a mountain cave, Destiny felt a presence drawing near. She closed her eyes and listened to the wind. After a moment, they snapped open and shone with surprise. Her child was close, and getting closer. She was sure of it. Its spirit, however, had changed—had become different from what she had felt just two days ago when she had found the girl.

Destiny thought again of the gryphons, and growled irritably. They had unfairly attacked her when her head was thrust inside the castle, questioning the girl. The audacity of those troublesome creatures! They dared to fight a dragon in her prime? She would have her revenge. Then Destiny thought of Gwendolyn. There was something in this girl that she had not sensed for many years. She reminded her of the ancient days when certain men stood before Destiny unafraid, even as she destroyed them—men who did not allow fear to rule their hearts but fought valiantly instead. Destiny had sometimes felt a grudging respect for them, and always greater satisfaction when she killed them. She had felt some of that satisfaction as she tortured Gwendolyn under her gaze. Before she could penetrate the girl's mind and force her to reveal the seed's location, however, she had been attacked by the gryphons and forced to flee. Even now, the area on her back where her scales had been torn away throbbed in pain. Fortunately, the injury was superficial. It hurt to use her wings, yes, but she could still fly. Her teeth and claws had grown no less sharp—and her breath was still deadly.

Then she felt her offspring's presence again. She should have been able to read his mind. Instead, it was closed to her. Why? She had to find out. Ignoring the pain in her back, she leaped into the air and flew north toward Ballan á Moor.

***

As the castle came into view in the late afternoon, Gwendolyn was surprised. There were no signs of Merovian soldiers swarming Ballan á Moor, nor even the town and farms that surrounded it. There was not even a ship in the town harbor. Where was the invading fleet? Then Kindle spoke.

"Look to the sea!" he cried.

They looked far beyond the shore and saw the wreckage of many ships floating calmly on the surface of the water. Ruined masts, oak barrels, rigging, planks of wood, and other debris were all scattered across the blue-gray sea as if they were a child's playthings. As they flew closer, they could see that a large sail attached to the main mast of one of the ships had somehow remained whole and continued to drift in the water. Emblazoned on the red sail was a black eagle. They all recognized Merovia's symbol instantly. Sköll's navy had been destroyed—and without a survivor in sight. But how?

Kindle circled over the wreckage when he saw something flying toward them out of the mountains.

He dove lower and glided several feet above the water. "Can you swim?" he asked, turning his head back towards Polonius and the children.

"Yes," they replied. Before they could ask what he meant by this, however, Kindle flipped over, dumping them into the sea. They yelled in surprise as they plunged into the cold, salty water. The next moment, Polonius and the children bobbed to the surface, unhurt, and looked up in confusion. What was Kindle doing? Then they understood. In the distance, another dragon advanced quickly toward them as Kindle raced south. They recognized Destiny's red scales almost immediately. "We must reach shore," cried Polonius. "Follow me."

Kindle felt his mother's thoughts as she approached. She was surprised and glad to see him—but her heart was full of hatred for all else. He could tell that she was injured by how she beat her wings unevenly. She forgot the pain, however, when she saw him. "How have you hatched without my breath?" she wondered. Then she saw three figures on Kindle's back. Humans. What was he doing with humans?

She flew faster towards him as he dropped them into the ocean. Instead of flying toward her, however, he streaked away south down the shore. Why had he not killed them? Was he playing with them like a cat does with mice? Where was he going? She tried to read his mind, just as he could read hers, but his thoughts were closed to her. She flew after him.

Kindle landed several miles away on the beach followed seconds later by his mother. "My child!" she cried. "Do you not know me?"

"Yes, mother," said Kindle. "I have felt your presence before." Now that he was face to face with her, Kindle was unsure about how he felt about his mother. He knew that she cared for him, but in a way that made him feel as if he were merely an extension of her. He also sensed her dark spirit—one calloused by murder and greed. When she had opened her thoughts to him, he could see in his mind's eye all of the horrible things she had done during her long, cruel life. She had killed countless creatures in her time—men, giants, trolls, gryphons, centaurs, and even other dragons.

"I have been asleep for many years, my dear," she said. "But I awoke to find you."

Destiny marveled at his appearance. Though he was only about half her size, his scales had already hardened, and his wings were strong and supple. When she had followed him along the coast she also noticed that he flew with a grace that had taken her years to learn. Destiny swelled with pride. He would be a powerful force beside her. Then a thought troubled her. "How were you able to hatch without me?" she asked.

"A clever human used the mountain's fire to wake me," he replied.

Destiny was surprised, then irritated. Was that possible? Who would dare to use her seed in such a way? No matter. She had found her child. Still, she would also find those who were involved, and make them suffer. "Men grow more intelligent every year," she grumbled. When she had discovered Kindle over the ocean, she had also seen the wreckage of the Merovian fleet, and assumed that he was responsible for its destruction. "One day they may rival us. We must kill them—all of them. You have done well by sinking those ships and eating those men."

"I didn't do that," responded Kindle. "Nor do I know what did. However, I do know this—men and giants can be honorable. I have fought alongside of them." Then he opened his mind to her for the first time and revealed his memories of the battle at Grimstad the night before. His mother noted Gwendolyn's courage in making peace with the giants after years of hostility.

"Your mind must have been poisoned by this girl," she hissed, angrily. "Peace? What peace do you want with them? You are a *dragon*. We *take* what we want and *kill* without apology. Why would you be bound by the laws devised by those weaker than you? Our breath is our only law!"

Kindle looked at her with pity. "It is not *my* law."

Destiny, however, wasn't listening. "Come with me!" she urged. "I will show you men as they are—weak, cowardly, and prone to betrayal. You will see how quickly they abandon their principles when they squirm in my grasp!"

Kindle thought back to the conversation that Gwendolyn had had with Ollom the day before. It had sounded like men and giants had once treated one another horribly. However, he had also witnessed great bravery and honor by both races in the short time that he had been with them. Perhaps most important, he remembered what he had experienced when he had shared Gwendolyn's thoughts as she put her hands on his shell. He saw that her soul was brave and kind. She was prepared to forsake his power forever. The thought of his mother killing her—and others like her—made him angry.

"I will *not* let you hurt my friends," he declared, with the hint of a growl. "Besides, torture would do you no good. They would never bow to you."

Destiny grew alarmed. Had they really corrupted his mind? She tried a different argument. "They will never accept you," she hissed, craftily. "They only pretend to be your friends now because they need your help. Once the danger is past, however, they will recognize you as a threat. Men and giants will corner you in a cave somewhere and kill you. You belong with your own kind."

"No, mother," replied Kindle. "I saw two races renew their bonds of friendship last night. Spirits can change. I've seen it. Let your spirit change too!"

Destiny's heart burned within her. First her seed had been stolen. Now she had recovered her child, but he had been poisoned by talk of forgiveness, reconciliation. She could not understand it. She had not survived this long by being weak. Her heart was strong and hard like a diamond. It could no longer be broken.

"I am asking you one last time," she said. "I have come for you—my flesh, my blood. Where does your allegiance lie if not with your family?"

Kindle raised his chin slightly. "I stand with the brave," he declared. "I stand with those who have faith that there is a higher purpose than hoarding gold, and a greater justice than the strong bullying the weak."

"Then you have made your choice," she said icily. "I do not say farewell, for you will surely be betrayed by those you call your friends. There are *other* seeds that I must awake."

Kindle looked at her in surprise. "*Other* seeds?"

"Did you think you were the only one?" she replied, scornfully. She turned and flew high into the air before disappearing over the horizon.

Kindle's heart was heavy as he watched her fly away. After what he had witnessed between Gwendolyn and Ollom, he had also hoped that his mother would be able to reconcile with men. That she could forgive them for stealing her seed—and that they could forgive her for her sins. Perhaps some things could not be overcome, he thought. He flew back and found Gwendolyn, Aethelred, and Polonius hiding at the base of the cliffs near the castle, shivering in their wet clothes. When they saw him reappear, they ran out to meet him.

"I'm sorry about dropping you so unexpectedly," he said. "I didn't have time to explain." He recounted his conversation with Destiny before she had disappeared. "I was not as convincing as you were last night, Gwendolyn. I will probably never see her again."

"Fine by me!" cried Aethelred, rubbing his shoulders to warm himself. "I've seen enough dragons for one day—present company excluded, of course." He smiled and looked up at Kindle nervously.

Polonius stroked his beard. "If Destiny didn't destroy the Merovian fleet, who did?"

Gwendolyn shook her head. "I don't know," she answered, softly. "But someone must have." Then she looked up at the dragon. "I'm sorry you couldn't change your mother, Kindle, but if you'd like, you can be part of our family now." She and Aethelred hugged him, and he nuzzled them with his head in return.

"If you're going to stay with us," declared Aethelred, "I think we need to build bigger rooms."

The dragon smiled. "That reminds me," he said, looking at the ruined castle. "Where are your people?"

"Oh! I almost forgot!" said Gwendolyn. She pointed to several long boats lying on the beach. "We found those." The markings in the sand showed they had been dragged on shore and left well beyond the reach of high tide.

"The footprints suggest a crew landed here a short while ago," explained Polonius. "They lead up the cliffs and towards the castle—or what's left of it." He looked up at Ballan á Moor. "Whoever commanded them should have answers."

Gwendolyn put her hand on the dragon's shoulder. "We were going to follow them but we waited to see what had become of you."

Kindle smiled. "Let's go find your parents."

***

They discovered that Ballan á Moor was still abandoned, but it didn't take long to find the refugees in the forest nearby. The people of Valmar had dug trenches around the camp's perimeter, and stayed busy by fashioning long spears out of tree branches. Argus had also ordered sentries to stand guard at various points among the trees to warn against invaders. Even though Wulfric and his crew had returned earlier and told them how the Merovian navy had been destroyed by the sea serpent, Argus remained prudent. As far as he knew, Destiny could still attack at any moment.

When one of the sentries saw Polonius and the children—followed by a dragon—walking towards him in the forest, he dropped his spear and ran. The children tried to call him back, understanding his fear of Kindle (while laughing nonetheless) but he had fled too quickly. Soon, they reached the camp, and they saw many men with sharp spears preparing to attack. Wulfric led the way.

"Stop!" cried Gwendolyn. "This is poor hospitality for the prince and princess of Valmar, is it not?"

The Valmarians were thunderstruck. Gwendolyn, Aethelred, and Polonius had returned beyond all hope! But who was this dragon? Where had they been? While Wulfric lowered his spear and continued walking toward them, Gwendolyn noticed that many of her people still held their weapons and remained where they were, casting doubtful looks at the dragon.

"This is Kindle!" she declared. "He has saved our lives more than once, and he is a friend of men. You need not fear him!"

More people lowered their spears as Wulfric ran forward. "My little warriors!" He picked the children up and hugged them warmly for a few moments. Then he put them down and inspected them, amazed by their appearance. Their clothing, torn and dirty, looked nothing like the fine attire in which he had last seen them. Nevertheless, the children both looked surprisingly well—except for a few scratches and bruises. Their faces, especially, looked older and more mature. Polonius, too, appeared healthy. He had much more energy than anyone would have guessed. So much had happened in such a short time that they hadn't had time to reflect on how often their lives had been in danger. Now the children collapsed into Wulfric's arms, and felt little again.

Then, over her uncle's shoulder, Gwendolyn saw her parents. They had come running out of their tent on the other side of camp when they first heard the disturbance. The queen looked horrible. She had dark circles under her eyes, and her hair, usually well combed and perfectly straight, was a snarled mess. Her father looked even worse. His face was pale and gaunt, and his eyes looked dead. When Argus and Thelda pushed through the crowd and saw their children safe, however, their eyes lit up. They ran to them and held them tight.

Once they had caught their breath, Gwendolyn introduced the dragon. "Mother, father," she said. "This is Kindle, the seed of Destiny. He saved our lives and now needs a family of his own."

The dragon lowered his head respectfully as the king and queen gazed up at him in wonder. "Your children have brave hearts," he said. "I am lucky to count them as my friends."

At first, the king and queen were too stunned to speak. They had never imagined a friendly dragon. Finally, Thelda found her voice. Wiping away her tears, she bowed low. "Words cannot express our thanks," she replied. "We are forever grateful."

"Yes," added Argus, bowing as well. "You are always welcome in Ballan á Moor."

There was much to talk about after this reunion. A meal was hastily made and, with the castle in ruins, everyone sat down for a picnic beneath the trees. Gwendolyn and Aethelred took turns telling their parents and uncle about their adventures. At first, Argus and Thelda had been quite upset with Polonius for taking the children from camp. They understood better why he had done so, however, as the children continued to tell their tale.

When it was revealed that Sköll had transformed himself into the boy known as Ghael, Wulfric grew red and slammed his fist into the ground where he sat. "Why did I trust that clever little brat?" he growled, shaking his head. The king, however, comforted his brother, telling him that they had all been fooled by Sköll's cunning, and that Wulfric had more than made up for it by helping to destroy the Merovian navy. (The children stopped and demanded that Wulfric tell them of that adventure, which he did.)

Everyone was also shocked when Polonius admitted to being part giant. "Now that we're allies once again, I hope that I'll be able to keep whatever remains of my library," he said, timidly looking over his glasses. Argus and Thelda had a good laugh at that, saying he was welcome but that because he had taken their children without permission, he would now have to split his teaching responsibilities with herding sheep. (Polonius chuckled at that, but then wondered if they were serious.)

Argus, Thelda, and Wulfric also shuddered as the children recalled the siege of Grimstad. They breathed a collective sigh of relief at the news that the troll army had been destroyed, and that Gwendolyn had brokered a peace between their races. The king quickly made arrangements to receive the giants when he learned that they would soon reach Ballan á Moor. "They will be happy there is no more fighting to be done," he said. "But they will be hungry from their journey." Remembering that giants considered blueberries a delicacy, he ordered his men to scour the forest to gather as many as they could find.

Finally, Kindle explained to everyone that his mother had returned to the land across the sea, and that they could safely begin rebuilding Ballan á Moor.

When the stories were finished, Argus stood and spoke. "Gwendolyn, Aethelred, Wulfric, Polonius, and Kindle, we are indebted to you for your bravery. It is perhaps well that most of our possessions have been destroyed, for I have no gift to give you that could possibly repay your valor." All of the people of Valmar cheered when he finished, and rejoiced at the thought of being free once again.

16

FIRE MEETS FIRE

It was now late afternoon, and the camp was busy with people preparing a great feast to welcome the giants, and celebrate their newly won freedom. The villagers had gathered many baskets of wild apples, strawberries and, of course, blueberries with which to greet their guests. In addition, the smell of roasting meat and fresh baked bread filled the camp. The Valmarians had even found a few barrels of ale that had survived the destruction of the castle, and now they tapped them with delight.

As preparations were being made, Gwendolyn and Aethelred took a long walk down the beach with their parents, talking quietly. Their father acknowledged that he had experienced the dragon magic as a boy, but he had watched his father, Edubard, wield it so ruthlessly that he vowed he would never use it himself. Soon after Edubard's death, Argus convinced himself that the magic no longer existed, and eventually he did not feel the power at all.

"I let my father's fears become my own," he said, as if speaking to himself. "I see that now." Then he looked at his children and his voice became merry. "But you have brought peace to Valmar . . . and to me," he added, smiling. "Our freedom has been won because courage, one of the strongest types of magic, still flows in our children's veins." Argus embraced Gwendolyn and Aethelred. It was wonderful to see their father this happy.

After a moment, Thelda put her hand on her husband's shoulder. "We'd better get back," she replied softly, dabbing tears of joy from her eyes. "The giants will be here soon and there is still much to be done." Aethelred ran ahead to chase a seagull while his parents slowly began to make their way back toward camp.

"Coming, Gwen?" asked Argus, stopping and holding out his hand.

Gwendolyn nodded. She turned and took one last look at the sea. The water was beautiful, peaceful, and clear. The thought of exploring it excited her. What adventures awaited her over the water? What strange new lands might she discover? She was just about to turn back to her parents when she saw something on the horizon. It was moving fast and low, but was much too large to be a bird. It could only be one thing.

She pointed across the water. "Look!" The others followed her gaze—and turned pale. Destiny had returned. Gwendolyn looked at her parents in desperation. "We must flee to the forest!"

"No!" cried her father. "We won't reach it in time." He looked about wildly. Then, a short distance up the beach, he saw some stone cottages that the fisherman used to store netting and tackle. "We must make for the cottages!" They all ran towards the modest structures, hoping to find a hiding place.

***

Destiny was still fuming as she soared above the clouds east of Valmar. She had come across the sea, enduring storms, gryphons, and the stink of men to seek her child. What had she found? Gratitude? Loyalty? No. A stranger. In fact, worse than a stranger. Kindle was now an adversary infected by human blood, human kindness. She could not let this pass. She turned and flew back, intent upon killing those who had corrupted him. And if Kindle chose to defend them? Well, she was prepared for that, too.

***

Kindle remained in camp talking to curious villagers, many of whom were still astounded that a friendly dragon was in their midst. Suddenly, he sensed something was wrong. He closed his eyes and knew somehow that Gwendolyn's life was in danger. But from what? Then he heard a distant roar and recognized his mother's presence instantly. He sprang into the air and flew toward the beach.

When he had cleared the treetops, he saw her. Beating her great wings, Destiny hovered over several stone cottages that stood on the beach. Then she opened her mouth and covered the cottages in flame, melting some of the walls. He sensed Gwendolyn and her family inside. They were all terrified—and Destiny was enjoying their fear. He lowered his head and streaked towards his mother.

She saw him coming, and prepared to finish him. They locked claws over the beach. Kindle's force pushed her backwards as they both beat their wings furiously to stay airborne. He felt stronger than his mother, but she had greater experience at fighting battles, including other dragons.

"Why?" he demanded. "They have done you no harm!"

"They exist," she responded. "That is enough!"

Kindle tightened his grip on her shoulders and beat his wings with all of his might, attempting to push her to the ground from above. He lowered his head and continued to drive her backwards, forcing her into the sand. But he did not see her tail. In a flash, it coiled around his neck, jerking his head backwards violently. Then he felt her teeth lock on his throat. They both crashed to the beach but her grip did not fail. If he chose to defend men, so be it. She would teach him what weakness was.

The pain made Kindle's mind spin. One of his wings had been broken by the fall, and with his throat caught in her jaws, he could barely breathe. He clawed desperately at Destiny's face but he could not free himself. The world began to fade. "Goodbye, my love," she whispered. "Your friends will follow you soon." Suddenly, a gryphon's scream could be heard in the distance. The next moment, Kindle felt the great jaws release him. He fell back on the sand, badly wounded and struggling for breath.

Gwendolyn peaked out from behind the shattered walls and saw two gryphons streaking through the air. Eldon and Khailen had returned. Destiny saw them too and remembered her wounds. She would not be surprised again. She sprang into the air with astonishing speed to intercept them.

Eldon flew directly toward her while Khailen circled to the dragon's left, waiting for Destiny to engage her mate before attacking from the side. The dragon, however, had seen this trick before. She pretended to chase Eldon as the other approached her right flank. Destiny, however, turned her head quick as lightning and covered Khailen in flame. The gryphon screamed as she fell through the air before crashing into the shallow surf below.

Destiny smiled to herself. With Kindle and Khailen badly wounded, only Eldon remained. Where had he gone? Had he fled? Before she could look behind her, Destiny felt something land on her shoulder, followed by a searing pain in her left wing. Eldon had torn one of her tendons with his great beak. She struck him with her tail savagely, and watched him fall to the beach—but the damage had been done. She could still fly, but only slowly, and in great pain. She landed to conserve her energy.

Destiny saw Eldon's figure on the sand a short distance away. Her kick had done more damage than she had thought. The gryphon lay on his side and moved his legs feebly near the stone cottages where Gwendolyn and her family remained hidden. Destiny watched, bemused, as Gwendolyn, Aethelred, and her parents emerged from the structure, trying to drag the gryphon to safety. But it was no use. The beast was too large and too injured to move. When Argus realized this, he placed himself between his family and Destiny, defiant and stone-faced as she approached. Destiny smiled in spite of her anger. These Valmarians were made of stern stuff. But no matter. It would make killing the girl and her family all the more pleasurable. She folded her wings and walked slowly toward them, trying to decide if she would eat them slowly or simply cover them in flame.

All of a sudden, the sound of horns could be heard in the distance. Destiny paused and looked behind her. Dozens of giants raced across the beach toward her in full armor, carrying shields and spears. Where had they come from? Was there no end to her enemies?

Forgetting Gwendolyn and the others for a moment, Destiny turned and faced her new adversaries. Ollom, king of the giants, led the way. He lowered his spear and picked up speed as he approached, followed by the others. Destiny roared in anger. Let them come, she thought. Not even the iron spears of the giants could pierce her armor. She rushed forward a few steps and launched a fireball at them but the giants crouched behind their great shields which deflected the flame.

Unfortunately for Ollom and his warriors, that was not Destiny's only weapon. Now that they were close enough, she swung her great tail, bowling over about ten of them. Even though they had used their shields to absorb the blow, the force of her tail sent them flying across the sand. Some of the giants got up—but others lay still. Then, despite the pain from her injuries, she leaped into the air and hovered over them. The giants raised their shields again and huddled close together, fearing her deadly breath. She, however, had something else in mind. She dove forward and snatched four of them up in her claws before carrying them high into the air. When she reached a great height, she simply let them go, and they fell screaming to their deaths.

She swooped back towards the group below, wincing in pain. Her wing hurt terribly but she was too angry to care. She made another pass, gathering up more giants, including Ollom. Though he thrust his great spear into her chest when she grabbed him, the weapon glanced harmlessly off her thick skin. She laughed at his foolishness and rose into the sky. Suddenly, she felt something clinging to her back. It was much too light to be a giant. Letting go of the others, she turned over in the air, twisting and writhing as she tried to shed whatever it was that clung to her. Try as she might, however, the creature remained stubbornly fixed to the scales between her wings. She climbed higher. If she couldn't dislodge it, perhaps the cold air might.

When Destiny had turned to face the giants, Argus never hesitated. He sprinted toward the battle, covering the distance quickly. All of the dragon's attention seemed to be focused on Ollom and his warriors when she dove into their ranks. Though she was stabbed again and again, their long spears seemed to have no effect on Destiny's great scales.

As she grabbed four of the warriors, however, Argus noticed that part of her armor between her wings had been torn away. When she approached the giants again, he knew that this could be his only chance. He picked up an abandoned spear and leaped, grabbing hold of her leg as she rose into the air. Showing tremendous agility, he scrambled on to her back with his spear still in one hand.

Destiny soon sensed his weight, however, and turned over abruptly to dislodge him—but Argus was expecting this. Clutching the deep grooves between her scales, he held on and watched as she released the poor giants from her grip. She continued to climb higher and higher into the air, whipping her tail back and forth. They were almost in the clouds now and he felt the chill of the coastal winds, which made it difficult for him to breathe.

So that was her plan, he thought, grimly. She would continue to climb until he lost consciousness in the thin air. Argus ducked as she flung her tail around, trying to knock him loose. He had to act quickly. Gripping the shaft of his spear, he found where her scales had been torn away. The area was thick and muscular—but he knew that iron was stronger than dragon flesh. He plunged his weapon into her back with all of his strength.

Destiny shrieked and fell like a stone, her heart skewered by cold iron. Argus let go of the weapon and smiled as he plummeted to earth beside her, knowing that this dragon could harm no one else. He hoped he would be remembered not as a king that allowed Valmar to be conquered, but as one who had helped give it back its freedom. He closed his eyes and waited for death as the wind whistled past him. Instead of crashing into the beach below, however, he felt two large claws grab his shoulders. He opened his eyes and saw Eldon looking down at him as the gryphon's wings fluttered overhead. The beast's hind leg was broken but he could still fly. A second later Argus heard a crash as the wreckage of Destiny's body landed on the beach far below.

The dragon was no more.

***

Kindle felt Gwendolyn's hand on his cheek and he opened his eyes. He had drifted in and out of consciousness during the battle. However, he mustered enough strength to focus on the girl who now stood before him. Unaware he was watching her, she busily tore strips of her dress, and used the material to staunch the puncture wounds in his neck. He noticed that she was crying. Then she felt his voice inside of her head.

"Thank you, brave one."

Gwendolyn stopped and looked into his eyes. "You're alive!"

"Yes," he replied, breathing with some effort. "I will live."

Khailen was not so lucky. Aethelred and Thelda dragged her burned and broken body from the surf and tried to revive her, but she was already dead. After Eldon had set Argus safely down on the beach, the gryphon flew to his mate with the last of his strength. When he saw Khailen's lifeless body, however, he lowered his head and wept.

Nearby, another figure also wept bitterly. It was Orion, Ollom's son. He had fought alongside his father against the trolls, and was proud to follow him into battle once again. However, the giants had thought they would be fighting Merovians on this day—not a dragon. When they had seen Destiny from the cliffs of Ballan á Moor, some hesitated, fearing they would find only death if they challenged her. Ollom, however, had only quickened his pace. Using the stone stairway cut into the cliff that descended to the beach below, he had sprinted toward Destiny, giving the rest of them courage. Though he had been slain, the king of the giants had distracted the beast long enough for Argus to climb upon her back and ultimately destroy her. Now, with heavy hearts, Orion and the others collected the dead, placing them on their shields and carrying them to the forest. There, they would stand vigil over the bodies for hours, as was their custom, before returning to Grimstad for the burial.

EPILOGUE:
THE WORLD IS A BIG PLACE

Once everyone had returned to the forest encampment, Argus and Orion talked in the king's tent, discussing the differences that had separated men and giants for so long. When they emerged, both leaders swore an oath, promising a new era of friendship and mutual trust between the two races. Orion then invited the king, queen, and the children to his crowning ceremony, which would take place after a proper time of mourning could be observed. Orion also said he would send many skilled stonemasons and metal smiths to help the Valmarians rebuild Ballan á Moor.

"But you have already given us so much!" Argus objected.

"No," said Orion. "We only return the kindness that Polonius, Kindle, and your children showed us by fighting on our behalf—though we did nothing to deserve their help." Argus could only bow, and thank the giants again for their generosity as they returned to Grimstad with their dead.

Everyone spent the next few days trying to recover from the damage that Destiny had wrought. The Valmarians set Eldon's broken leg, following his instructions, and marveled at how quickly his bone healed. Soon the gryphon said that he had the strength again to fly (though he would continue to limp for quite some time). Nevertheless, he insisted on carrying Khailen's body high into the mountains where he would bury her. Before Eldon left, the king and queen thanked him for his help, and begged him to return so that they could reward him with rich gifts once the kingdom had recovered. The gryphon, however, simply shook his head.

"Keep your gifts," he replied, gruffly. "I am not a dragon—and have no desire for gold." Then his eyes softened. "Besides, I have already received my gift. It is the peace that you have made with the giants. See to it that you don't give that away too easily!" Picking up Khailen's body, he flew away deep into the mountains.

Then there was Kindle. His wounds were quite serious, and he had lost a good deal of blood as he lay on the beach. He remained there for a few days, still too injured to move, while Gwendolyn, Aethelred, and others brought him meat and water. Strengthened by the food—and by the children's love for him—he was finally able to walk to camp where he took refuge in the forest's cool shade. There he rested, and as he healed, Kindle earned the respect and the trust of the Valmarian people with whom he spoke.

Shortly after Kindle came to camp, Argus ordered Destiny's body burned on the beach. The people heaped great logs of oak and ash around her corpse before setting the pile on fire. It smoked dreadfully but the ocean breeze quickly blew the terrible smell away. The only trace of Destiny's remains was a scorched area of sand.

A week later, Argus gave orders to have the camp dismantled. The Valmarians returned to Ballan á Moor to rebuild the castle, the town—and more slowly—their lives. As Kindle became stronger, he worked alongside the townspeople, helping to clear the site by picking up large pieces of stone and debris. Now that the danger was over, everyone worked enthusiastically to restore the village, and talked of how they would make it bigger and better than before.

Though his wing would take months to heal, Kindle wasted no time learning about his new home. When their work in town was over, he and the children took long walks through the forest in the early evenings as he learned where the Restless River would freeze over during winter, where the sweetest wild strawberries grew, and where the best trees were to climb. He asked many questions, but the children were very patient with him, especially when they came across a dead boar and he ate it raw on the spot. He was, after all, still a dragon.

***

One day, as Gwendolyn and her brother sat on the beach watching the sunset, she felt a longing again in her heart to explore the sea. It was, however, no longer a frustrated desire. With Sköll dead and their independence assured, the Valmarians were now free to sail wherever they wished.

Uncle Wulfric was already making plans to rebuild the navy, using the money that he and his crew had gained as pirates. He told the children that they would be the first ones allowed on board the new ship he was building. Polonius, meanwhile, had recovered some of the books and maps from his library, and was already showing Gwendolyn and Aethelred areas that had never before been explored. Finally, the king and queen promised the children that they could accompany them to the Moaning Isles to re-establish trading ties.

As Gwendolyn and Aethelred talked quietly together one evening, snacking out of a picnic basket nestled between them, they saw their father approach. "Come along!" he called, cheerfully. "It's almost bedtime."

"Coming, father," they replied, rising. Then Gwendolyn had a thought. "Can't we continue north once we've visited the Moaning Isles?"

Argus shook his head and chuckled softly to himself. Gwendolyn had never left Valmar's shores, and already she wanted to explore areas that even he had not visited. "What do you think you would find if we continued to sail north?"

"I don't know," said Gwendolyn, excitedly. "I've heard fishermen speak of fish as big as oak trees that breathe air like we do; and islands with black sandy beaches; and coral reefs larger than our forests—and stranger things besides."

"The world is a big place," Argus acknowledged. "Something tells me you will explore much of it in the years ahead—but not today. Have you forgotten that we leave for Grimstad tomorrow to attend Orion's crowning?"

"Oh!" exclaimed Aethelred, looking into the basket beside him. "That reminds me. We need more blueberries. They'll be disappointed if we don't bring any with us!"

Argus looked puzzled. "You and Gwendolyn gathered more than I could count yesterday," he said. "What happened?" Then he noticed the empty basket sitting between them.

He smiled. "Well, I suppose you'll find more, tomorrow." Gwendolyn and Aethelred grinned, revealing blue-stained teeth, as they walked back towards the castle, hand in hand with their father.

ACKNOWLEDGEMENTS

The following people helped to make this book possible.

John planted the seed.

Megan drew the pictures.

Judy, Anne, and Robin tamed the words.

Rachel told the truth.

Thank you.

ABOUT THE AUTHOR

Roy Sakelson lives with his wife,
two children, and a cat in San Jose, California.

www.roysakelson.com

16772745R00137

Made in the USA
San Bernardino, CA
19 November 2014